RAINBOW'S END

RAINBOW'S END

James M. Cain

W. H. ALLEN · LONDON
A division of Howard & Wyndham Ltd
1975

Printed and bound in Great Britain by
Butler & Tanner Ltd, Frome and London
for the publishers W. H. Allen & Co. Ltd,
44 Hill Street, London WIX 8LB

ISBN 0 491 01525 9

RAINBOW'S END

1

It was the same old Saturday night Mom and I had been having off and on since my father died—or at least the man I had thought was my father. Here lately, the evening got started earlier than it had been starting, as the filling station where I worked was closed, with the sign hung on the pump: "Sorry, No Gas." So there I'd be, home with Mom. But don't get the idea that things were slow or that time dragged. Plenty was going on, a little too much, for my taste, and too lively. The first part—in the early evening—wasn't too bad, just screwy, which, of course, there's no law against. She'd begin talking about how rich we would be by and by, pretty soon, one of these days, and tonight was extra special on account of the rainbow she'd seen late in the afternoon, after the rain when the sun came out.

"And you know, Dave," she whispered, "what's under the end of that bow—a pot of gold, that's what. It's waiting for us, I can feel it—if we just show some gump. If we take the car next week, go out there and get it."

"There's a road to the end of that bow?"

"You know what I mean."

"No, I don't."

Because she'd meant so many things at one time or another, I'd more or less lost track. Like for a while she meant oil, insisting it ought to be drilled for on our land, and then we'd get royalties on it, "thousands and thousands." I told her southern Ohio was all drilled out. "They used to have oil here," I explained, "but that was years ago, and there's no more to be had—on our land or any other." Then for a while she meant Marriott. She'd read about Marriott in the papers, that he should locate a park on our land, with roller coasters, ferris wheels, and on the river a steamboat ride.

Our place is on the Muskingum, ten miles up from Marietta, or two places, actually—small farms next to each other that we grew produce on, she doing most of the work, me helping her when I could, with hired labor when we needed it. It's true that steamers once ran on the river, but I didn't know any way of getting Marriott up here. She'd meant other things too, each one goofier than the last, so what she meant now I didn't exactly know, but I let her tell me; I knew I'd have no peace till she did.

"OK, what is it?" I asked.

"Well," she began, drawing a long, trembling breath, "this time it can be done—by us. We don't have to ask nobody. We just up and go—drive over in our car when we get good and ready to take advantage."

"Of what?"

"Because this time we can—"

"Will you for God's sake say it?"

8

"It's in Maryland. We drive over to Cumberland, which is less than a day's trip, and—"

"Yeah? And what?"

"Buy us lottery tickets."

So, all that puffing and poofing, and she comes up with this. But she was small and young and pretty in her freckle-faced mountain way, and I knew by then that she lived in a world of dreams. So I kissed her and told her: "Fine, we'll drive over to Cumberland—that's the place?—next month when the roads dry off. Right now, everything's flooded, and we'd be up to our hubcaps in water. But soon as it goes down we'll go and buy ourself a ticket."

"More than one, Dave—we have to buy a bunch. That way, you're bound to win."

That wasn't the way I'd heard it, but I went along and for a while kept her company pretending. Then after a while I asked: "So OK, we cash a ticket—then what?"

"Well, we'll be rich."

"I asked you: *and then what?*"

"Then . . . with all that money we could sell this place, sell the other place too, and sit back and—"

"And what?"

"Whatever we want."

We had two places because I'd bought a second one after my father died—her husband, I mean—in addition to the place we had when he was alive. That place he had built himself in the only way he knew—with a hammer, saw, lumber, and his two hands. A ranchhouse, he called it. He was from Texas, and when he went into the army, he had been put on recruiting duty in Marietta,

9

where she was slinging hash in a lunchroom. She was from Flint, West Virginia, then a coal camp on the Monongahela, now a ghost town, with the mine closed down, though a strip crew has started work on the other side of the mountain. She'd worked first in Fairmont, down the river from Flint, but she got let out after a row she got into. That's when she crossed to Ohio. I asked her once why she came so far instead of picking Clarksburg which was just down the road. "I don't like Clarksburg too well," she told me, but once when I was over there I found out the reason. She was a Giles, and back of Clarksburg the place is full of Kings. A Giles doesn't come near a King, on account it's not healthy. I'm trying to explain her a little, how being "mountain" caused her to be like she was.

So they got married, she and Jody Howell, and he bought the other place with the money they'd both saved and built the house himself. He built it the way he knew from Texas: square, cut up into four rooms with connecting doors, two front doors, two back doors, a front porch, and a kitchen out in the back yard. However, a house that's perfect for Texas is cold as death in Ohio. When winter came, we almost froze. When I was 16 he came down with galloping TB and sat out on the porch all day with a cup beside him to spit in, "chasing the cure," as they call it. Then he died. He had never told us he carried insurance, but a check for $10,000 came, made out to me. With the money I made a down payment on the place next to us, $9,000 against the price of $22,000, and we moved to the new house. She was bitter toward him, that he carried insurance for me, "and not one cent" for her. That's when it started up, her acting so peculiar, which is what I'm leading to. I'm not going to apologize for beating around the bush a little bit; the way I feel about it, I could beat around the tree, even a whole forest full of trees.

OK, then, I'll say it: she made passes at me. After talking about the gold, the money we would make one way or another, she'd catch hold of my hand, pull it around her, and draw it across her breast that was full and warm and soft. It scared me to death and then some. I've been trying to say she was mountain, and I'd heard of stuff like that—of mothers that fell for their boys, and vice versa, fathers and daughters.

It sounds funny, but you have to remember that mountain boys of 16 can load just as much coal as pappy, so when they work in the mines, they get married, mostly to girls of 14, maybe younger. Well, when Sonny comes sweet 16, never been kissed, a goodlooking boy with muscles, mommy's still in her twenties, with ideas no older than that. And of course it kind of works backwards, with pappy and Sissy, soon as he notices her. I'm trying to say when you run into something like that, that you hardly dare to believe, you generally find there's a reason. With Mom, there was her looks on top of her age. She was still in her thirties, and I was just 22. She was medium, verging on small, with dusty blond hair, light blue eyes, pale skin, and freckles, and a body no man could forget.

But I'm still beating around the bush. I'm trying to say: what scared me to death was that if she was mountain, I was too or at least so I thought. It turned out I actually was, though in a different way than I'd supposed. If I was mountain, maybe I wanted my hand

11

to be there as much as she did. I had a horror about it, that we might be headed for something like going over the dam nine miles down the Muskingum.

So all of a sudden I said, "Time for bed." We both slept on the first floor of the new house, me in the den, her in the dining room. The way the house was laid out, the front door opened onto a hall that led back to the kitchen, and that had stairs in it, leading up to the second floor and a closet under the stairs, for wraps. To the left of the hall, through an arch leading in, was the living room, with a fireplace at the far end, and a double door in the rear wall, leading to a dining room. Beside the fireplace was a door to a small den that was built as kind of an annex to the living room, but mainly to make a sundeck up on the second floor. To get us all on one floor, she had me sleep in the den and put herself in the dining room, both of us on cots she bought in town, and under blankets, as she said sheets were "just foolishness" besides being trouble to wash. I felt pretty ashamed but went along. So this particular Saturday night I was no sooner tucked away than there was a tap on my door, and there she was, bringing me cornbread and buttermilk. I drank and ate while she sat beside me in nightie and blue kimono, but with everything hanging open, unbuttoned. I said: "Hey, pull that kimono together!"

"You've seen me often enough. It's just nature."

"I've seen you too often, especially here lately, and maybe it's nature, but that's not saying it's right."

"You mean, on account of my being your mother?"

"What do you think I mean? And why don't you mean it?"

"There might be a reason, Dave."

12

That's the way she always talked about it. She always slid past the point, never hitting it on the nose, so it didn't occur to me she might mean something actual. I told her: "Goddamn it, pull that thing together!"

"Did you hear what I said?"

"Did you hear what *I* said?"

She pulled it together at last. Then, as though it was just a funny idea that had popped in her head, she said: "You look so comfortable there in that bed, I wouldn't ask much to crawl myself in right there with you."

"I wouldn't ask *anything* to kick you the hell out. Here, take this glass and git."

I drained it and handed it over. She took it and said: "You aren't very nice to me, Dave."

"You're too damned nice to me."

"Little Davey Howell, listen—"

"I said git. So git."

At last she got or git or whatever you'd call it, and after I'd snapped off the light, I lay in the dark asking myself, what about it? There was no doubt what she meant. The question was, what did I mean? I was 22, with normal impulses, a little too normal these last two months, since a girl I'd been going with left me flat, turned around and married a guy for no reason at all I could see except that he had a Cadillac. It had rocked me pretty hard, especially at night, which was when that girl and I got together for some great lovemaking. With Mom, I thought my answer was no, but I wasn't sure that it was. I lay awake and was bothered plenty. But I must have gone to sleep, because I woke up all of a sudden with the light shining in from the living room,

13

and Mom by the bed, shaking me. At first I thought it was more of the same.

"Dave," she whispered, "there's somebody down on the island. They're hollering."

The "island" was a little hummocksy hill in the river that had stuck out from the east bank where we lived and then had been cut off by the river a couple of years before. It was in sight of the ranchhouse where we kept a light burning to make it look like someone was there. It wasn't in sight of this house, though, unless you went upstairs to look.

"Mom, you're imagining things. No one could be on the island. There's no way on this earth they could get there. It's probably some drunk on the road, wanting help with his car. Now go back to bed. Leave me alone; let me sleep."

"Maybe no way on this earth. There could be other ways."

"Other ways? What are you talking about?"

"What do you think?"

Then suddenly I remembered the newscasts, the flashes they kept coming up with while we were watching TV about the plane a guy had hijacked by holding a gun to a girl as his hostage, a stewardess on the plane, and making it fly all around in a crazy way, from Chicago to Pittsburgh and back and around, while $100,000 and a parachute were brought and handed over—with 28 people on board and a storm coming up. Mom stood there in the half-dark, staring down at me, and whispered: "He's hollering and she is too, that girl—she must be the one he was holding the gun on—it's got to be that."

I jumped up and ran back to the kitchen and listened. Sure enough, I could hear a man yelling, and then in between a girl.

"OK," I said. "We have to go down. Get the flashlights while I put something on."

2

She was already dressed, waiting for me out back. I put on my pants and shoes but no socks and a sheepskin coat, without a shirt. In the kitchen I picked up the rifle that always stood there. It was an Enfield from World War I my father had got at a surplus sale in Marietta. I threw the bolt and rammed a round into the chamber. With both of us holding flashlights, we went down the path. As we got near the water's edge, the guy stopped hollering and all of a sudden said: "Hey!"

"Hey," I answered. "Who are you?"

"Never mind who I am. You got a boat?"

"Johnboat, yeah."

"You got a car?"

"Yes."

"Get the boat. Show me the car. Hand me the keys."

"Oh please," the girl cut in in a trembling voice, "do what he says or he'll kill me."

"OK, OK."

"You heard me, kid. Do it now!"

"And you heard *me*, I hope," I said. "OK, but there's a couple of things we have to get straight first. Lady, who are you?"

"I was the stewardess on that plane, the one he hijacked last night. He kept holding a gun to my head. Then when they finally opened the door, he was too scared to jump, and I pushed him. He grabbed me, and we both went. He kept hitting me to make me let go, but I wouldn't, and then we came down in the water. Oh, please, he could kill me *now*. He—"

"Oh no he won't."

"What makes you think I won't?"

"If she gets it, you do too."

No answer to that, so I told him: "You can't get off that island without me ferrying you over. God help you in that water if you try to swim. It's flood tide. They'll fish you out dead nine miles down when you go over the dam. Understand?"

"Yeah."

"Yeah, what?"

"Yes sir."

"OK. Now I have to get oars from the house—"

"What house?"

"Over that hill."

"I don't see no hill."

"I'll have a light put in."

I said, "I'll be back with the boat" and started for the house, whispering to Mom: "Whatever I do, keep talking." By now she had turned off the spotlight. I went on up to the house and into the kitchen to look at the clock. It said five after five. Daybreak was only a few minutes away, so I had to move fast. I went outside again, picked up the oars from the back porch, and went down the other path to the boat which was tied up to our little landing. Fortunately, a week or ten days before, I had put it up on a trestle.

It takes a few days for a boat to swell after being out of water that long, and of course it leaked, but not much. The second time I had bailed it out there wasn't much to bail, which meant it was tight and ready. So, after stripping off the tarp I had put on, I was ready to go. A johnboat is a square-ended thing the size of a soap dish, with a seat in the bow, one in the stern, and one across the middle. I got in and tilted one oar and the rifle on the seat in the bow, using the other oar as a paddle. Then I shifted the shot bag from cuddy under the front seat, to balance my weight, and cast off. The shot bag was a sixty-pound canvas bag full of buckshot to trim the boat with when I went out alone. Then I sat down on the seat in the middle, holding onto the landing. With the river being so high, the boat was less than a foot out of water, which, of course, made it handy. Then I waited, watching the sky in the east. Down below I could hear voices, yelling—Mom's, the guy's, the girl's—the girl's loudest of all. I had no idea what she was yelling about, but if she was yelling, she wasn't dead. So far, so good.

The sky was beginning to turn gray, so I shoved off. I shot the boat out into the stream and started to paddle. It was a left-handed way to go, but I didn't dare row regular, on account of the noise it would make, the thump of the oars in the oarlocks. I rounded the point. Sure enough, Mom was there on the bank talking. I steered to bring the hummock, the little hill that was part of the island, between me and the guy and the girl. I feathered the oar to swing in close and let the current carry me. I came to a tree, one sticking up out of water where the river had risen around it in the spring flood we were having, and caught it. Suddenly all three voices came through, the girl yelling at Mom: "Do you want him to kill me? Is that why you dare him to do it?" And Mom yelling at her: "I'm trying to get through his head what'll happen to him if he dares do it, that's all I'm trying to do!" And the guy telling Mom: "OK, OK, but I goddamn well might; I might blow her head off if she don't shut up and you don't!"

That made no sense at all, but I'd told Mom to keep talking, and if that was her idea of something to say, I couldn't stop her now. I pulled the boat in a foot at a time, to jam it against the tree with one end on the bank. I could just see the guy, silhouetted against the sky. I picked up the rifle and aimed it at him. "Drop that gun," I said, very quiet-like.

He didn't. He whirled and shot. I heard the *whack* of the bullet as it cut twigs over my head.

He cursed as the recoil lifted his gun, which was a small one. It couldn't have been more than a cheap .32.

I still had his head in my sights and squeezed the trigger.

The flash lit up the island, and suddenly he wasn't there.

"Oh thank God, thank the merciful God!" sobbed the girl, coming suddenly into view toward me. But after a few steps she fell and started moaning about her feet. "They're all cut up!" she said. "The river took my shoes."

I tilted the rifle back in its place against the front seat, hopped ashore, and ran to her through the bushes.

19

She was half-sitting, half-lying against a stump, her teeth chattering, and moaning. I whipped off my coat and put it on her, telling her: "Hold on to me now, give to me when I lift." I put one arm around her back, the other under her knees, at the same time kneeling myself. Then I got to my feet and carried her to the boat. "I'm so cold, so cold, so cold," she whispered.

"Take it easy," I said.

I helped her to the seat in the stern. This time, instead of paddling, I set the locks in their holes and rowed. I pushed clear of the tree, backed into the current, and let it take me below the island. Then I pulled for the east bank, shooting the bow up on it right beside Mom. I jumped ashore, gave the painter a hitch on a tree, and helped the girl ashore. But her feet still flinched at each step, and I picked her up once more, this time not having to kneel. "Get the rifle, will you?" I told Mom.

She didn't answer or even act as though she heard me. She gave the girl's hand a jerk and yelped into her face: "What'd he do with the money?"

"Who is this crazy bitch?" screamed the girl. Then without waiting for me to tell her, she exploded at Mom: "How would I know what he did with the money? How would I know what he did with *anything?* All I know what he did with was what he did with that gun, thanks to you trying to get him to shoot me, daring and daring and daring. Didn't you know he had to be nuts? Didn't you know he just might have done it—killed me, like you said? Didn't you know that all that crap you dished out about what might happen to him if he shot me meant nothing to him at all? Hey, I asked you something! Why did you do that to me?"

"Get the rifle," I repeated to Mom.

"I'll bring it!" she snapped. "But first I'm going out there, going out and having a look."

"Have a look at what?"

"The money, that's what."

"What do we have to do with that?"

"A reward'll be out for it. They always pay a reward! If we turn it in, we can claim it."

"Mom, you leave things lay."

"I will, except for the money."

"If I can put in a word," said the girl, touching Mom on the shoulder, "you could take off your clothes and start diving down in the river. It got everything—his parachute, his hat, my shoes."

"How do you know it got his hat?"

"He kept talking about it."

By now it was full daylight, and Mom kept staring at her. Then: "OK," she said to me, "take her up to the house and give her some clothes to put on. There's some old ones of mine in my bottom bureau drawer."

"Mom, use some sense."

"And don't you call no one, Dave, till I give you the word."

"I have to call the sheriff."

"But not till I give you the word."

I still had the girl in my arms. At last we could start for the house. After two or three steps she whispered: "I'm sorry to be so much trouble."

"You're no trouble."

"Am I getting heavy?"

"Not to me you're not."

"Mom? She's your mother?"

"That's right."

"I took her for your wife."

"I don't have any wife."

"I'm sorry I yelled at her, but she almost got me killed."

"She gets some funny ideas."

"Dave? Dave what?"

"Howell. What's your name?"

"Jill. Jill Kreeger."

"Pleased to meet you, Jill."

"Likewise."

A wan smile crossed her face. By then we were on the back porch of the house. Her arm suddenly tightened, the one around my neck. That brought her face against mine. She kissed me, first on the cheek and then on the mouth. "Hey, hey, hey! Jill, will you open the door?"

She reached down and turned the knob. We went through into the kitchen. I kicked the door shut behind me, then carried Jill up the hall and through the living room to the den. I was ashamed of the bed, all mussed up with only blankets on it, a pillow without any case and no sheets. But she didn't seem to mind, dropping off my coat and getting ready to jump in. But she had on those soggy clothes, such as they were—short red pants, a red bolero, as she called it, and some kind of thing like a bra. I stripped them off her quickly. She was standing in front of me, naked, a beautiful thing to see. I banged open a bureau drawer, grabbed a towel, and rubbed her dry, then bundled her into the blankets. But in the cold air of the room with no clothes on, her teeth started to chatter. "I'm having a chill," she said.

"Hold everything!"

I started upstairs to the bathroom, but ducked back for one more kiss. She wanted it too, but her lips were cold as ice.

3

Upstairs I tried the water. When it was hot, I left it running while I went back to Jill. She was still in the bed, shaking. I wrapped the blanket around her, knelt by the bed and lifted, and carried her up to the tub. I took off the blanket, so she was naked again, and smacked her one on the tail.

"Get in and get in quick."

She did. She stretched out in the hot water and for a second the chattering went on. Then it stopped and she closed her eyes.

"OK?"

"Yes, it's heaven."

"Is from this angle, no kidding."

"Am I pretty?"

"Beautiful."

"I want to be, for you. . . . Know what you looked like? From my angle? Out there just now?"

"I'll bite. What?"

"God."

She said it low and solemn. I didn't gag it off or make any answer. After some time, she said: "Well? You always heard that hell's hot, but you find out that cold can be worse, especially wet cold, with a rotten guy holding a gun to your head and a crazy, screwball woman egging him on to shoot. Then a voice behind you speaks. Then a rifle goes off. And from being down in hell, you're in heaven all at one swoop. How would he look to you, the guy that flew you up there?"

"Like he needed a shave, I bet."

She touched my chin and said: "God wears a beard, too. I'm sure he does. It shows in all the pictures."

"OK, but I couldn't tell you what would show in a picture of you. It would be against the law."

She slapped water over the things I was talking about and asked, very innocently: "You like them?"

"I love them."

They were round, with the nipples all spread out in the hot water, and beautiful. She slapped along, then said: "They're floating up—to you." At last I dipped my hand in the water and cuddled one, and she whispered: "It took you long enough."

"I didn't have the nerve."

"God's not supposed to have sex appeal, but let Him learn how to shoot and He can look awful pretty. I should have said, I was praying. All the time out there I was praying. Then when you spoke from the boat—"

"I'm not God, I'm Dave Howell, and I know you're getting to me."

"Then it's mutual."

"Hold still, I want to look at your feet."

They were small and cute and pretty, but when I felt

them she started to squeal. "Stop!" she yelped. "That tickles."

"They're not cut, that I can see."

"They hurt outside."

"That underbrush would hurt. . . . They may be bruised a bit, but they're not cut."

"OK."

She sat up, cut the water, soaped under her arms, sloshed herself, then came back to the subject of Mom : "Dave, why would she? Egg him on to fire that gun? She didn't even know me. Why would she want me killed?"

"You must have misunderstood her. She's *mountain.* We're a peculiar bunch. We always say it opposite."

"Listen, maybe I could misunderstand her, but not my belly. My belly knows what she meant. But why?"

I didn't have any answer to that. The way Mom had acted had also baffled me. I said "Let's forget it" or something like that and tried to get back to us.

She said: "OK, but you better be going down. She could come any time, and better you not be up here."

"OK. Kiss me."

She kissed me very solemnly but pulled back all of a sudden. "Why hasn't she come?" she asked. "What's she doing out there?"

"What's it to us what she's doing?"

But Jill kept staring at me. Then at last she whispered: "I know what she's doing: she's swiping that money, that's what. She said she was going to look for it, and that's what's keeping her there. *And that's why she wanted me killed.* Once he killed me and you killed him, you could roll us both in the river and who would know where we died, or when, or who shot us? You could stash that money and keep it. You—"

"Hey! Quit talking like that's what I wanted—"

"Dave, I didn't say *you* wanted me killed. I don't believe you did. Just the same, if I *had* been killed out there, if I *was* dead, you'd have had to go along. You'd have had to play it the way she wanted, because after all, she's your mother—roll me in the river, roll him in, and keep the hundred thousand."

"You *do* have it figured out, don't you?"

That's what I said, but I have to own up—she shook me. The way Mom had acted out there by the water's edge had a mighty peculiar look.

Jill kept staring at me and then went on, pretty cold: "Well, all I've got to say is, if that's the mountain way, I'm glad I was born lower down. Is that all they know, just go around killing people?"

"Sometimes it has to be done."

She kept staring at me, then all of a sudden closed her eyes as though hit with a whip. Then she reached out and touched me, gripping my hand in hers. "I'm sorry, Dave, I forgot who's God, that's all. I won't again, ever. . . . Yes, sometimes killing a guy can be the most glorious thing in the world." Then: "You have to go down."

She pushed her wet face to mine but once more pulled back and asked: "What's she *doing* out there? Why hasn't she come? She also has that gun. If she gets here before you call, my life's not worth a plugged dime. Dave, you're calling, you're calling that sheriff *now! Now*, do you hear? *Now!*"

27

I didn't believe her life was in danger, but with a beautiful, naked girl beside you, dripping water and banging you over the head, you do what she says, if for no other reason than to make her shut up. I went down-stairs, looked up the sheriff's number, and called. The officer who answered sounded sleepy. I didn't get much reaction even when I mentioned I'd killed a guy "to save the life of a girl." But when I mentioned Shaw, the hijacker of that plane, the officer came to life fast. He told me to wait till he got his pen, then told me to "start over," and "say it slow while I write it down." When he had the name, time, and place all straightened out, he checked over what he'd send out: an ambulance for Jill, a "dead wagon," as he called it, for the body, and "anything else?" he asked, very friendly. I couldn't think of anything, and he said: "The officers'll be right out, soon as they can get dressed. Hold everything till they get there." I said I would.

As I hung up, Jill came limping into the room, the blanket wrapped around her. She asked to borrow the phone, which was next to the arch out in the hall, and I got up to let her sit down. By the number of spins on the dial, I knew she was calling long distance. When the answer came, she said: "Jack? It's me, Jill." Apparently the guy all but dropped dead, because she cupped the phone and whispered: "It's Jack Mullen, our chief dispatcher. He thought I was dead, and it's kind of knocked him over." Then she was on the phone again, telling him what happened over and over: "Be sure you call Mr. Morgan right away now, quick. Tell him I'm all right. Thank him for sending the money, and give my best to Mrs. M. She's a doll, and she was worried sick

28

about me. I would call them myself, but I don't have their number with me because it got dunked with everything else I had. And give them my love; be sure you don't forget that." Mr. Morgan seemed to be president of the airline.

She hung up and said: "Well? Now I feel better!" That was when Mom came in, carrying the rifle. Jill said: "Mrs. Howell, I'm sorry to tell you, Dave has called the sheriff. So if you figured to· shoot me, it'll cost you twenty years in Marysville, so maybe you better not."

"No one's planning to shoot you," I told her, kind of short. I was getting fed up about something she had no proof of and that I didn't at all believe. Mom paid no attention to her, but said to me: "I can't find no trace of that money. What he done with it I don't know, but could be he slipped it off, slipped off the straps of that poke, when he unsnapped the parachute. I found *that* all right. It's out there in the river, on the other side of the island."

"It don't concern us, Mom."

"You sure you didn't find that money and hide it?" Jill asked her sarcastically. "You've been out there long enough."

If Mom made a pass with the gun, I don't know. Maybe she just thought about it. Whatever she did, Jill caught it and flinched in her chair. "I'm taking that," I told Mom, reaching for it. But she backed away, and I had to get tough to make her give it up. She kept saying: "Leave me be. This gun's mine. It belongs to me. Your father bought it for me, so I'd be protected." That was news to me; I thought he had bought it for himself.

"Whoever it belongs to," I snapped, now pretty

disagreeable, "it's evidence in a killing. It has to be handed over to the police."

At last I had it and could put it on the living room table, the low one in front of the fireplace. "I think it's time for breakfast," I said, and to Jill: "Could you stand some food?"

"I'd like some coffee, please."

"Coming up."

Generally I did the cooking, but this time I took Mom out to the kitchen with me to get her away from Jill—and away from that gun. The stove was electric. After I'd got out the kettle and filled it, I snapped on the coil under it and got out my grill that I used for fritters. It was stainless steel, twelve by twenty-four inches, with bolt holes around the edges. I bought it in a junkyard. What it had been part of, I don't know—the floor of a truck maybe. But for me, once it was greased with Crisco, it was perfect for top-of-the-stove frying, like fritters. I greased it up now and cut the corn off the cobs, starting the bacon first in a heavy skillet I had. Soon as the kettle started to whistle, I made coffee and took it to the living room on a tray, with a napkin, sugar, and cream. Pretty fancy. Mom didn't bother to hide her disgust. I put it on the table in front of Jill. She put in four lumps of sugar and some cream and started to gulp, flinching in between from its being so hot. Suddenly she looked like a half-starved child, and my heart went bumpity-bump. I made quick work of the orange juice, eggs, bacon, and fritters, but ate mine out there with Jill while Mom ate in the kitchen. Every so often I'd pat a strong little hand and it would pat me on the cheek. I'd just got through washing the dishes when the doorbell rang. I opened the door and there the officers were.

4

It seemed the sheriff was in Europe on some kind of business. The officer who was in charge was a sergeant named Edgren. He introduced himself and then the deputy with him, a middleaged man named Mantle. He also introduced, or pointed at, the intern on the ambulance, who had pulled up in back of the sheriff's car, a doctor named Cline, and the undertaker, Santos, who was getting out of the "dead wagon," a black, enclosed truck with no markings of any kind, that had pulled up behind the ambulance.

Sergeant Edgren asked me: "You killed a man, that right?"

"The hijacker, Shaw, yes."

"You identified him already?"

"The girl identified him. The one who came down with him on his parachute."

"She here?"

"Right inside."

"She's the one that's to go? In the ambulance?"

"She'd better go, sergeant. I'd say she's in pretty bad shape."

"Dr. Cline?"

Dr. Cline came up with two men who got a stretcher out of the ambulance, and I led the way inside. When I'd introduced the whole bunch to Jill, she motioned to the blanket and started talking like she was used to taking charge. "Pardon my informal clothes," she said, very cool, "but my others got wet in the river, where I came down on the parachute. Mr. Howell fixed me up with this blanket."

Dr. Cline touched her forehead, felt her pulse, and made a face. His men put the stretcher down, lifted her on it, and carried her out. As they were sliding her into the ambulance I bent down and kissed her. "You get well," I whispered.

"For you I will."

Edgren was at the door keeping an eye on me. As soon as the ambulance drove off, I went back with him. "OK," he said. "Start at the beginning."

"Not much to tell. However—"

So I told it, beginning with Mom's waking me up, the walk to the water's edge, the argument there with Shaw, my trip up to the landing, my paddling down in the boat, my order to drop the gun, the shot he took at me, and the one I took at him. "That killed him, at least, I think it did. I didn't look, but I imagine my mother did. You can talk to her about it."

"When was this?"

"Little after five. Twenty after, I'd say."

He opened a notebook and glanced at it. "You called us at six after six."

"Something like that, yes."

"What took you so long? What were you waiting for?"

"I had that girl on my hands. She was in awful shape from the cold after coming down in the water, fright from his holding that gun to her head, and shock at seeing him killed. First things first. She was important. He could wait."

"Your mother was there, you say?"

"That's right."

"Why couldn't she have called?"

"She was looking for the money."

"What money?"

"The money the airline put up. That was put in a zipper bag with straps to go over his shoulder, so it said on TV. That he had on him—that he must have had on him—when he jumped with that parachute."

"What she have to do with it?"

"She wanted to claim the reward."

"For what?"

"Sergeant Edgren, from what the girl had told her, the water took everything when they came down in the river—his hat, coat, shoes, the girl's shoes—everything they had, including, of course, the money. But my mother thought it just might have floated after he threw off the strap, after he swam to the island, and that if she got going real quick, if she rowed out there and looked, she might be able to grab it before it sank, before it got waterlogged, or got knocked to pieces below, going over the dam. So you can't call from a johnboat. So that's why she left it to me."

"She find it?"

"I'm sorry to say, she didn't."

"Where's he at now?"

"Where he fell—on the island."

I led them around the house and down the path to

the boat. "That's him," I said, pointing. "Over there in the bushes."

I offered to row him out, but he motioned to Mantle who pushed the boat in. Then the two of them—Edgren in the stern, Mantle at the oars—rowed out to have a look. "OK," he told Mantle. "Load your camera. You got work to do." Mantle snapped film into his camera, then got busy, shooting pictures of the corpse, measuring with a steel tape Mantle had on a spool, taking note of the trampled underbrush, and so on. Then Mantle called to me, wanting to know where I had been, "when you fired the shot that killed him."

"I'll show you."

They rowed to shore again, and I stepped in the bow of the boat. Mantle headed downstream, then to the island's far side. I had him pull for the tree and caught it, just as I had before, and pulled the boat in to jam it, exactly the same way. All three of us got out and headed for the stump where I'd picked up Jill, which was four or five feet from the corpse. Mantle spotted a twig, a fresh one on top of a bush, and looked at it with a glass. Then he wrapped it in a Kleenex and put it in his pocket. "I think," I said, "it was cut off the tree by his shot."

"That's right," he agreed. "It's important. More or less proves you shot in self-defense."

The three of us got in the boat again and rowed back to the bank. Edgren said: "I broke Shaw's gun, found one empty shell in the chamber. The rest of it, one twig cut off the tree, apparently by his bullet, corresponds with what Howell said."

"You mean, write it up that way?"

"It all checks out."

"OK."

So we were done except for moving the body, recovering the parachute, and impounding my gun for evidence at the inquest that would have to be held. Mr. Santos refused to put the body on my boat. "We'd just be asking for trouble. If that thing should capsize, I've got two men in the river, we don't mention that body, and God knows where I come out. You'll have to call DiVola." DiVola was a fire company down the river that had a bigger boat, an aluminum thing with an outboard. To call them, we all went back to the car, the sheriff's car with a dashboard phone, and Edgren did his talking standing beside the door. But as we walked around the house I could see Mom inside, talking on the phone. I knew right away who to. It was Sid, her brother over in Flint, who got in it deep before long. Of course, she had to tell him about it, but right away I began to worry.

I've already mentioned her left-handed way of talking. If she should get in it now and began telling it in a way that didn't match up with what I'd said, and especially what Jill would say, if they ever got around to her, it could all get loused but bad. So I was nervous while Edgren talked, and hopeful when he hung up, that we'd be going down to wait for DiVola, but I was too optimistic. He had hardly turned around with the news "they're on their way," when the door opened and Mom was there. I hardly knew her. Her hair was all combed up with a blue ribbon on one lock, and her face was powdered to hide the freckles. She had on light tan pantyhose and her best blue dress, which was short, to show her goodlooking legs. Everyone turned, but she

35

didn't speak at first, just stood there staring at Mantle. Then: "Well, Mr. Mantle, howdy," she sang out very friendly. "It's been a long time, hasn't it?"

But Mantle gave a blank stare. Then: "Madam, do I know you?" he asked in a puzzled way.

"You certainly do," she told him. "I'm Myra Howell, Myra Giles that was—Little Myra, they called me, to tell me apart from my cousin, Big Myra Giles, who's two years older than I am. Mr. Mantle, I'm the girl that bit that bandit! Remember?"

"Oh! I place you now! And later, you were the girl Mr. Hanks called us about."

"I'd like to forget that if you don't mind. Why, the idea, him calling the police about an argument two girls had. I never thanked him for it."

"You were smaller then."

"I was only sixteen. I grew. You moved to Marietta?"

"I'm from Marietta originally."

"But you're working for the county?"

"Sergeant Edgren has some questions."

I could feel the drawstring pull on my stomach, but she talked so simple and honest and natural that even I believed her. She told how Shaw had "made passes at that girl, poking the gun at her head and her stomach and ribs, and all the time saying he'd kill her. And then my son spoke to him from the other side of the island, and I couldn't hear what he said, but at the sound of his voice the man spun, spun around on one foot, and let go with his gun. Then I heard my son's gun, and he dropped to the ground. And soon as my son brought the girl, took her ashore from the boat, I knew I had to get moving, to bring in that poke full of money, the one they were talking about on TV. So when Dave had gone up with the girl, I got in the boat again and rowed out to the island, first to have a look if he was really dead, and if he was, to pick up the money and bring it in. He was, all right, with his brains scattered around, but no money was there. Then I remembered the parachute he'd come down with, and thought if it was still in the river, the poke with the money might be tangled in it. If I got out there quick I could grab it before it sank from water soaking in. So I rowed around to the other side of the island and found the parachute. It's caught on the bottom somehow, between the island and the bank on the other side. But I couldn't see a poke. It could be there, though, if someone got out there quick and fished up the parachute. It could be tangled up in it."

It all matched up, not only with what had happened but with the way I'd told it myself—so much so that even I believed it in spite of what Jill had said. Yet Mantle kept looking at her, and the drawstring didn't loosen. When she started all over again, about how scared she'd been for "that girl," I wanted to beg her to stop, to leave well enough alone, but of course, I didn't dare open my mouth. Just then a horn sounded from below. That shut her up, and we all went down to the river.

5

———————•———————

When we got there the DiVola bunch was out on the island, having a look at the corpse—three firemen in helmets and plastic coats, their boat tied to a tree, a smaller one than the one I had braced the johnboat against, but sticking out of the water the same way on account of the rise in the river.

Mr. Santos called out to them: "If you'd put one of those helmets on him, kind of hold his head together, he wouldn't be so messy to handle." One of them looked up and said: "Hey, that's a good idea. How about us using your hat?" That seemed to take care of that, but Mom chirped up real friendly: "You can wrap his head in a towel. I'll get you one from the house."

So she went legging it back, looking quite pretty in her dress and a coat she'd put on over it. She came back with a bath towel, but while she was gone they had it, back and forth from the island to the bank, about how they were going to do it. They decided to put Shaw in the firemen's aluminum boat, which was maybe 16 feet long, with an outboard on the stern, but instead of using the motor, to put it in tow of my johnboat, with Mantle at the oars and a fireman in the stern, holding the bow of the skiff. They thought that would be better than using the motor, as it was only a hundred feet from island to bank, and oars would give better control. So, soon as Mom got back with the towel, that was how they did it, first tying Shaw's head up, mumbling every second about what a mess he was. Then while one fireman got in my boat to grab the skiff, the other two picked him up and loaded him on. But by that time he was stiff, with his arms sticking up in the air, not a pretty sight, especially with the towel wrapped around his head.

There they came, bringing him in: first my johnboat with Mantle rowing and the fireman in the stern, then the skiff with one fireman in the bow, the third fireman in the stern, and Shaw stretched out in the middle with his arms sticking up. Mantle did a real neat job of pulling in to the bank, and Edgren grabbed the johnboat's front end to hold it, while I grabbed the bow of the skiff. We tied both boats to small trees. Then Santos' men stepped up with a stretcher like the one Jill had been put on and loaded Shaw on it, covering him with a blanket, though his arms still stuck up. Then they took him away. Edgren told Santos: "Put him in storage, but don't freeze him. I'll call the coroner myself, and he'll take it from there. He'll be having an autopsy done, and there'll have to be an inquest."

"Sure, sure, sure."

Santos seemed to know about what would have to be done and followed his men up the path. Mom said: "Aren't you looking for that money?"

"You know where is?" asked Edgren.

"Could be tangled up in that parachute. I know where *it* is, but I tell you right now, if you do find that poke, I'm putting in for the reward. I got it coming for showing you where to look."

"We got nothing to do with that."

"With that poke? Why not?"

"With the reward."

"I want my cut, I'm telling you."

"Tell the airline, ma'am."

Mantle helped her into the johnboat, manned the oars again, and rowed around the island, first downstream a little way, then up on the other side, until they were out of sight, hidden by the bushes. "Hey!" he called out. "Here's the chute, looking at me."

"OK," Edgren told him. "Hold everything. We'll be out."

But he and the firemen had to figure out how they'd do it. They finally decided that the motor was out again; the propeller would foul in the parachute's cordage. Then they saw they would need a line to tow the chute in with and asked me if I had one. I remembered a light cotton rope I used to line things up when putting in corn. When I got back from the house with it, Mantle had rowed Mom back to the riverbank again. She was giving out once more about the reward. Nobody made any comment. Then Mantle rowed around the island again, up to where the chute was, caught on some snag in the river. The firemen had oars in their boat and followed behind the johnboat. Then Edgren, Mom, and I walked up the bank a short ways, past the head of the island, so we could see what was going on. One of the firemen reached down in the water, fished some cordage up, and made my line fast to it. Then they tried to haul the chute into the boat, but it slopped things up so bad that they gave up and decided to drag it. They rowed over to where we were, paying out my line as they came, and then started to haul. It was slow work. Out there in the johnboat, Mantle kept having to clear the cordage, when it would foul up. He would lean out of the boat, and once almost capsized. At last, though, he got things clear. The chute came out on the bank—silk with red and white pieces. It was no sooner on the bank than Mom started pawing at it, "in case that poke is in under it," she said. But it wasn't, and she nearly cried. "That means it's in the river," she wailed. "Being swept down to go over the dam. If it ever gets in the Ohio, we never will get it back! *Never!*"

Mantle kept staring at her, and Edgren asked my permission to spread the chute on my land, "to give it a chance to dry." I told him, "of course," and the firemen spread it over some bushes. It was now around nine o'clock, and I asked them all up for some early lunch. "I can give you hot dogs pretty quick," I said. "With coffee and pie. They might go pretty good."

The sheriff's men had to go back, however, and the firemen were due downriver. They said goodbye to me and Mom, then putt-putted away. Going back to his car, Edgren told me and Mom: "We'll be out later on in the day to ask more questions about it—if that girl is able to come. Around five o'clock, I'd say. So stand by. If you want a lawyer, you're entitled to have one, and of course, if you don't want to talk, you don't have to."

"Well why wouldn't I want to talk?"

"I'm advising you of your rights. You killed a man. I don't think you'll be charged, but you might be. It's not up to me to say."

"Who is it up to then?"

"Coroner's jury—they generally do as the state's attorney says. But if we have reason, we can charge you too."

"And that's why I need a lawyer?"

"I didn't say *need*. You're entitled to one if you want him."

"Well, that's nice," said Mom. "Here my boy kills that awful man, and now you're fixing to lock him up."

"Ma'am, I'm not fixing to do anything, except what the law requires, and right now the law requires I advise him. Which I've done." And to me: "You understand, Mr. Howell?"

"I think so. Thanks."

"And ma'am, you were a witness, so you must stand by, too. You're entitled to a lawyer, and you don't have to talk if you don't want to."

"You mean I could be charged too?"

"It could happen."

"With what?"

"We don't know yet."

That's what he said, but before he said it he shot a look at Mantle who didn't return it but kept his eyes on the ground. "Well I like *that*," said Mom.

"Any questions?"

I didn't have any. If Mom did, she kept them to herself, so the officers drove off—but not till I got them the rifle which they took with them, the empty shell still in the chamber.

6

We went in, and Mom said: "Well, thank God it'll soon be over, and then the sun will come up. Won't it?"

"Well? It generally does."

She had plumped herself down on the sofa and looked at me kind of funny as though what I said wasn't quite what she expected to hear. But before she could say what that was, a car turned in to our lane from the main highway and pulled up in front of the house—a cream-colored truck with the letters on the side of the TV station we have across the Ohio from Marietta at Parkersburg, West Virginia. Then a woman was ringing the bell and guys were getting out. She wanted to come in and take pictures of me and Mom, and I said OK—"but the real star of the show was that girl, Jill Kreeger's her name, who rode that parachute down, and held Shaw off somehow until I had a chance to plug him."

"Oh, but we have her already."

It seemed that Jill was hardly in her hospital room before they were there too, "and shot her in her nightie, the short one the hospital gave her, which wasn't much of a costume, but a lot they'll care tonight, when the tape goes on TV. That's a mighty pretty girl, and the tribute she pays you, Mr. Howell, is really something to hear."

Mom didn't say anything.

They set their camera up at the end of the room, next to the arch, and the woman put me on the sofa, using the low table, the one in front of the fireplace, to sit on herself. Then she began asking questions. I answered as well as I could, though there wasn't much to say, and I felt she was disappointed. I strung it out as well as I could, how I carried Jill to the house, "got her into a hot bath, to stop her teeth from chattering, and then called the sheriff's office." After a while she seemed satisfied, then decided to work on Mom. That made me nervous, for some reason, but when she'd put Mom on the sofa in the place where I'd been sitting and stayed where she had been, there on the low table, it began to go all right. Mom really gave out with it, all about her "doing my best, to get it through his head what would happen to him if he dast to kill that girl." You'd have thought Mom was the star of the show, and the woman was suddenly delighted. Then Mom blurted out: "But my boy is the one—except he didn't tell it right. We're mountain, and we don't brag about what we do. But when the time comes to do it, we do it—as he done."

You could tell how pleased the woman was, and I was doubly pleased, from having my worry eased. Then she and her crew left, and Mom kept asking: "Was I all right?" I told her she was and patted her cheek, but right away I wished I hadn't. She grabbed my hand and kissed inside the palm in that sticky way that she had. But the sound truck was hardly gone when a little Chevy showed up with three reporters in it—one from the *Marietta Times,* one from a Chicago paper, and one from some news service, maybe the Associated Press. They had cameras with them and took our pictures. Then they began asking questions, one of them with a recorder, so we had to start all over. By now Mom was doing it big and this time gave out with all kinds of stuff about how she'd looked for the money, "and pretty near drowned out there, when that johnboat all but tipped over——because I don't swim, not a stroke." Then they left, and once more I felt relieved, though what about I didn't quite know.

Then some people came in with a ham all cooked up, potato salad, baked beans in a casserole, and a can of shrimp—"as we know how busy you must be, and some lunch will come in handy." But what they really meant was they wanted to hear about it. The radio had carried the news, at least that I'd killed Shaw, so the girl was safe. They were from a couple of miles upriver. At that time of year, nobody lived very near us. There were houses on both sides of the river, but of summer people who locked up their places in winter and hauled their boats out on trestles. So I put out some of the ham, beans, and salad, and Mom told it again, this time about finding the chute. But right in the middle of it, around one o'clock I would say, the phone rang. When I answered, it was a lawyer I know whose car I had gassed often and who seemed to like me. Fact of the matter, I thought he was responsible for me being picked to follow Mr. Holt as manager of the station soon as he leaves for California next summer when he retires. Bledsoe was his name. I knew from the tone of his voice he had something on his mind.

"Dave?" he asked very sharp. "Are you alone? Are you free to talk?" I told him: "Not right now, I'm not. Can I call you back?"

"Make it quick, Dave."

He gave me his home number, and the people who could hear got the point and left. When I called him back, he said: "Dave, I heard something just now that may mean nothing at all, but on the other hand, it may mean plenty. But first, how do things stand with Edgren?"

"Well, he was out—he and a deputy named Mantle. That's his righthand man, apparently. He told us to stand by, that's all."

"For what?"

"Further questioning."

"Yes, but when?"

"Later on today—five o'clock he thought. If the girl is able to travel."

"Yeah, the girl. She's what I'm calling about. Dave, I had a call just now from Rich Duncan, a client whose car was stolen, or so he thought. He'd reported the theft to the sheriff's office. Then when he found his daughter had taken the car for a weekend with the boyfriend at a motel over in McConnelsville, he called me about what to do. So I told him get in there fast, to sign whatever papers they had, so the girl wouldn't get picked up and land in the middle of something. Which he did, so, of course, the sheriff's clerk was on the phone, and Rich suddenly realized what the call was about—you, the dough, and that girl. The clerk kept repeating over and

46

over again, to the prosecutor apparently: 'Mantle knows her from way back and wouldn't believe anything she said on a whole stack of Bibles.' He kept saying it over and over, and then wound up: 'Mantle, he can't shake off the idea there's something funny about it.' So, Dave, here's what I'm getting at: I want to be there—today—when the questioning resumes. Don't worry; I won't charge you a cent. I owe you something, the whole county does, for what you did today. Besides that, you've been damned nice to me. So—?"

I told him, "OK, and thanks," real quick, to cut it off, because the thing of it was, of course, that who Mantle had known wasn't Jill but Mom. We set it up that he should come around 4:00, "so we can check it over," as he said, "what we're going to say, so at least we all say the same thing."

"What was that all about?" Mom asked when I'd put down the phone.

"Lawyer I know named Bledsoe. He offered to come out, and I let him."

"What do we want with a lawyer?"

"Just to be on the safe side."

"You're keeping something from me." In some ways, Mom resembled a bobcat more than a human being, because a bobcat knows just by looking at you what you're thinking.

I said: "I'm not keeping anything from you. He told me: 'After all, you shot a guy, and you can't be sure what Edgren's going to do.'"

"I don't like that Edgren, and I don't like that Mantle."

"Yeah, him."

"I don't like him at all."

"What happened with him in Fairmont?"

"Nothing."

"He was on the case of the guy you bit. What other case was he on? And where did you come in?"

"You want the story of my life?"

I kept at it and pieced it together: in the place where she worked, another girl had accused her of stealing her tips, and the manager had called the police. Mantle at that time was on the Fairmont force. Nothing was done, and she got on the bus for Marietta. This took me an hour to find out and didn't tell me much, but at least it explained Mantle and what he thought about her.

I washed up the dishes after the lunch I'd given our visitors. Mom helped but bumped me quite a lot over and beyond the call of duty. It was nearly 4:00 when a car pulled up outside, a Chevy, but nobody got out. When I went out, Jill was on the front seat, dressed in nurse's clothes, but without a nurse's cap. A nurse was on the back seat and a guy was at the wheel who I'd never seen before. Jill introduced me to the nurse and to the man, Mr. York, who, it turned out, was with the airline Jill worked for. He had been rushed on a plane by the airline president within a half hour of her phone call and had hustled down here with money and whatever else she might need—like this car he'd rented for her, "as long as I want it—I never felt so important in my life."

"Baby," he told her, "you're the heroine of the year. Maybe Mr. Howell saved you, but you saved 28 lives. We don't speak of a multimillion dollar plane. That was due to break apart in the next air pocket unless that door

48

could be closed. You pushed him out, thank God. I hope you feel as important as we think you are."

"Well, who am I to say no?"

"Anyhow, come in. All of you."

"David, until the officers get here, I'd rather wait in the car."

"Why?"

"I have a reason."

It wasn't hard to guess what the reason was, and I didn't argue much but stood by the side of the car, talking through the window, with the nurse leaning forward to hear and Mr. York speaking up now and then. In a minute or two another car drove up and Mr. Bledsoe got out. I introduced him, and he took off his hat politely and said: "Let's go inside."

"When the officers come," said Jill. "If you want to go in Mr. Bledsoe, please do, but we're staying here—"

"I said, let's go in," Bledsoe snapped. "They'll be here any minute, and we have to talk—*now!*"

"Well, who are you," snapped York, "to be telling this girl what she does?"

"James J. Bledsoe, attorney at law, representing Mr. Howell. I suggest that Miss Kreeger accept me as counsel too. She's in trouble and time is running short."

"Trouble?" said York. "*Trouble?* Here she's the heroine of the year and you try to say she's in trouble."

"If Mantle says so, she is."

Jill drew a blank, looking first at me and then at York. "Who's Mantle?" he asked.

"I think she knows."

"What's this about?" snapped Jill. "What in the hell's it about? I never heard of Mantle."

By that time I was nudging Bledsoe who was staring at Jill. I took him aside and whispered: "She's not the one Mantle knows." Suddenly he backed water, apologizing as hard as he knew how, but insisting all over again that Jill "could be in trouble" and begging her to come in, "so we can get together on what we tell the police when they come."

Jill looked at me. When I nodded, York saw me do it. He whispered something to her and she said: "OK." But she flinched when she put her weight on her feet, and once more I carried her. She put her right arm around my neck.

7

I introduced Mom who took charge. She pointed at the armchair for Jill, the sofa for me and herself, and various chairs for the nurse, York, and Bledsoe. But I set Jill down on the sofa, camped beside her myself, and let everyone else, including Mom, find places where they could. Bledsoe got to the point at once: "Let's get going. What's Mantle suspicious about?"

"What ain't he suspicious about?" asked Mom. "He's a rat. He suspicions everyone—for no reason."

Bledsoe eyed her, comprehending at last what his friend had heard on the phone but hadn't rightly got the point of. But when he looked at me, I sidestepped. "Well, I wouldn't know," I faltered.

"Dave! You do know. Spit it out!"

"The little he said," I told him, "he seemed to think it funny I killed Shaw around 5:30 and didn't call in until 6:00. I explained to him the shape Miss Kreeger was in, how I was actually afraid she would die—"

"I would have," she cut in.

"Well, she could have," said the nurse. "She was in

dreadful shape when we got her. She's in pretty bad shape *now*."

"Why didn't *you* call, Mrs. Howell?" Bledsoe asked. "Did Mantle go into that?"

"I explained it to him over and over," Mom answered. "That I was out looking for the money, to find it and claim the reward. I started looking right off, and that's why I didn't call. It wasn't my fault it wasn't there. I found them the parachute, though—a lot of thanks I got."

Bledsoe thought this over and asked: "Is that what you told Mantle?"

"Edgren did the talking."

"Edgren, then?"

"What else was there *to* tell him?"

He thought some more, then asked me: "So what's Mantle suspicious of? Or Edgren? Or whichever it is?"

"I don't know."

"Come on, Dave, let's have it."

"Perhaps I might know," Jill said. "They think she stole the money while pretending to be looking for it."

"Were you here, Miss Kreeger?"

"No. They hauled me off in an ambulance before the questioning started. I just think that's what it was. If I can think of it, they can think of it."

"Well, thanks, Miss Whatever-Your-Name-Is, thanks a lot. Here I save your life and you up and call me a thief."

"You *are* a thief."

"Don't you call me that! Don't you do it!" And with that, Mom jumped up and ran at Jill. Jill rose from the sofa, waited till Mom was close to her, then let go with a slap that banged Mom down on the floor. I was blocked off by the table, but Bledsoe helped her up and led her back to her chair. "You rotten bitch," snarled Jill. "You tried to get me killed, you—"

"Will you cool it!" bellowed Bledsoe. "We have just a few minutes. Are you going to use that time to save your necks or to send all three to prison? Don't you realize that that's all it takes? That the three of you start working against each other, to land you all in the soup?"

"Not me, I don't think," Jill told him, kind of waspish.

"Especially you, beautiful you."

"For what?"

"Conspiring with Howell and Mrs. Howell to murder that guy for the money. If it's ever found, God help you—and especially God help Dave Howell."

"Why especially Dave Howell?"

"He pulled the trigger on Shaw."

There was a long, dark silence. Then York strolled over behind the sofa. He leaned over Jill, gave her a pat on the cheek, and said: "Honey, he could be right. Perhaps—it's up to you—but I was sent here to help however I could, and I feel I should say what I think. Perhaps you should take it easy."

Her face twisted up and she said nothing. Nobody said anything and a minute or two went by to the sound of Mom's sniffling. Then two more cars pulled up outside, one behind the other.

Edgren and Mantle got out of the first car, and a guy I didn't know, but who looked like a college professor, got out of the second. When I stepped outside and Edgren introduced me, I knew who he was: Mr. Knight, of the state's attorney's office, the one who handled big homicide cases. He was pleasant enough, but it was Edgren who took charge when I brought the three of them in and introduced Knight to Jill, Mom, and the nurse, whose name I don't remember. He knew Bledsoe and spoke to him pleasantly. I got some dining room chairs from Mom's room, then we were ready to begin. Edgren led off with Jill, "Advising you of your rights: You don't have to talk unless you so desire. You're entitled to counsel, who may sit in with us now."

"Mr. Bledsoe is my counsel."

"You want to talk or not?"

She turned, before answering that, to Mr. York, who squinched his eyes and said: "Just you don't get excited."

She looked at him, at Bledsoe, and at Edgren, then said, "OK."

"So," Edgren said, "shall we begin at the beginning?"

"Where's that?"

"The plane, I would say."

"OK, but I don't like to remember those hours with that idiot waving his gun around and making them take us from Pittsburgh to Chicago and back, all the time explaining he liked me personally but would kill me just the same unless they did what he said, 'exactly, exactly, exactly.' He kept saying it over and over, like some kind of football yell. Then, once he strapped on his parachute, after making me stand with my back to him, over the money that they brought in a bag and that he strung over his shoulder by its canvas strap, he yelled into the first-class cabin: 'Everyone down! Lean your head on the seat in front!' When everyone did, he made me walk ahead to the passenger exit and made Lefty Johns, who was our copilot that night, open it.

"But then he lost his nerve. He looked out and couldn't jump. That's when we hit the air pocket and dropped I don't know how far—couple hundred feet at least. Two or three women screamed. I'm used to air pockets, and it wouldn't have bothered me, except that the whole plane creaked and I knew all of a sudden, that with the door open like that, another drop could tear us apart. Lefty knew it too because he yelled at Shaw real loud: 'If you're going to jump, jump! Will you for Christ's sake jump!' or something like that. But still nothing happened. Shaw just stood there looking out, a scared look on his face. When the plane creaked one more time I spun him around and pushed. But he grabbed me to keep from going out. Then the two of us were spinning down through the night, him hanging onto me and me hanging to him. Then I remembered the ripcord and found it and pulled. I was almost shaken off when the parachute opened. Then, like in some horror movie, I was over my head in water, but water so cold it stabbed inside me like ice. I screamed, but when the water went down my throat I cut it off quick. Then I came up and could see what looked like shore, with bushes and stumps and trees against the sky. I swam to it, but when I crawled out and stood up, it hurt my feet horribly. The water had taken my shoes off, and I was in my stocking feet. Nothing on but my pantyhose and my skirt, bolero, and bra—but they were soaking wet."

"Wait a minute," said Edgren. "You're now on that island out there?"

"I was and he was, soon as he climbed out beside

55

me—but we didn't know it was an island then. He was the one who found it out after circling around. He still had his shoes on and could walk. Then he turned on me, blaming it all on me, saying that we were 'trapped in this God-awful place' and saying that he would kill me. For that, he began drying the gun, blowing into the barrel and rubbing it on his trousers to get the water off. Then he saw what looked like a house, with a light showing upstairs."

"That was this house?" asked Edgren.

"I don't think so."

She turned to me and I started to speak, but Edgren cut in with his speech about my rights. Bledsoe then motioned to me, and I explained about the other house. She went on: "He yelled at it and so did I. I'm here to tell you I did. Then two flashlights came over the hill, and Mr. Howell was there with this lady."

"Just a second," said Edgren. "While this was going on, while he was drying the gun and while you were yelling at the house, did he still have the money?"

"Sergeant Edgren, it was dark. I couldn't see. It was cold, so cold. All I could see was that gun—but I couldn't rightly see that. When he jammed it against me, sometimes against my head, I could feel it."

"Did he mention the money at all?"

"Not as I recall."

"Didn't blame you, or something like that, for its being lost in the river?" That was Mantle, getting into the discussion.

"He said nothing about it at all."

On that, Edgren, Mantle, and Knight put their heads together, and Bledsoe looked at me. I knew what he was thinking: that Knight and both officers thought it peculiar that if Shaw *had* lost his money, slipped it off when he unsnapped the parachute, he wouldn't have mentioned it to her, to blame her for it, as one more reason for killing her or at least to start to search for it. But when Edgren resumed, he told her: "OK, take it from there. Mr. Howell came with his mother. What then?"

"Shaw asked, did he have a boat, and Mr. Howell said yes. Shaw said, go get it or he would kill me. So he left and Mrs. Howell started hollering at Shaw and he hollered back."

"About the money? Or what?"

"Why the money?" asked Bledsoe. "How did that get in this?"

"It's what Mrs. Howell said she was thinking about at the time."

"Repeat the question."

"What was she hollering about?"

Jill looked at Bledsoe, at York, and at me, at me the longest, then said: "Sergeant, with a gun jammed to your head and your teeth chattering from cold, you don't pay too much attention to what's being said by a woman you can't even see a hundred feet off in the dark. She was arguing with Shaw, that's all I remember now, but what about, I have no idea."

She made the rest of it short, how the voice said "drop that gun," how Shaw had whirled and fired, how a rifle spoke, how Shaw had dropped at her feet, "his brains running out of his head." She told then how she'd started for me, "and fell on account of my feet," and how I'd come "piling through the bushes, put his coat on me, and carried me to his boat. I'd been praying to God, and

57

I don't mind saying right here that he looked to me like God. How do you like that, he still does."

She put her hand in mine and there was a kind of pause. Then Edgren asked: "What then?"

"How do I know, what then?"

There was another pause, and she said: "He carried me to the house, and this lady mentioned the money, said she meant to start looking for it. I think that's what she said. I had my mind on that coat, Mr. Howell's heavenly coat—though it left him bare to the waist."

She mentioned the bed, the bath, and my call to the sheriff's office, then remembered her call to Chicago, but didn't say anything about the brawl we had had when Mom came in with the rifle. Edgren pressed her about how much time had gone by between Shaw being killed and my phone call, and she guessed a half hour. "Long as it took to roll me into that bed, then put a blanket on me and carry me up to the bathroom, then dunk me in the tub."

"One other thing," said Edgren. "How did this man, this Shaw, get his gun past the metal detector? Did he mention that while you were with him on the plane?"

"You'd like to know, wouldn't you?"

"I think everyone would."

"Well, you work on it, mister. You won't get it from me. If I tell you that and you tell everyone because they want to know then we start all over on this hijacking thing. How he did it was so simple anyone who has 10 dollars could do it. Yes, he mentioned it, he bragged about it. But he's dead now, and I'm not telling you or anyone."

8

That seemed to be that, and York came over to give her a pat on the cheek. Edgren asked if I had anything to add to what I'd said that morning. Then he turned to Mom who said: "I got plenty to add, to officers who I try to give some help and they treat me like a thief. But outside of that, nothing. Not at all." Mantle cut in to say that she hadn't been treated like a thief or any other particular way, and she said: "It's what I'm talking about—and especially, nobody's thanked me for the help I've tried to give."

"Thanks a lot," Edgren said.

But Knight cut it off by motioning the officers over for a huddle. That's when Bledsoe knelt in front of Jill, beckoned to Mom, and whispered to the three of us, but with York still standing behind Jill. "I think," he whispered, "the officers want all three of you held. That time lag after the shooting still sticks in Mantle's mind, and that, coupled with Mrs. Howell's acknowledged interest in the money, must set up the possibility in his mind that Dave Howell plugged him for the money while his mother and Miss Kreeger cooperated. I think that's what they're whispering about—and Knight is naturally reluctant to face that judge when I move to have you released on bail. But why let it come to that? I can settle the whole thing now, I'm pretty sure, in one very simple way. Now look me in the eye—all three of you—and give me a straight answer. Is there any reason, any reason at all, why this place shouldn't be searched? And that other place, too, wherever it is?"

"No reason I know of," I told him.

"Of course there's not any reason!" exclaimed Mom. "What reason could there be? Do *you* think I'm a thief, too?"

"Well, I certainly know of no reason," Jill told him.

He stood up at once and called over to Knight: "Marion, the officers, I suspect, still have their minds on that money—and think Howell held up his call so his mother, Miss Kreeger, or he himself, could hide it. That being the case, they want the place searched, this house and the other one, *now.* They'll waive a warrant."

"Well?" said Knight, looking first at Edgren, then at Mantle. "That does it, I think."

"OK?" asked Bledsoe.

"All right, let's go."

So the two officers searched. I'd heard that a search turned your place upside down, but that's not how it was that day. Both officers knew their stuff and went through the place fast, leaving things just as they found them, first downstairs, then up on the second floor. That surprised them plenty, because nothing was up there except for linen in the two bathroom closets. I showed them the stairway to the attic. "There's nothing up there," I assured them, "at least, as I think. To tell the truth, I only looked once."

They made it quick, then we got in their car to drive to the other house—down the lane, maybe a quarter mile, to route 60, then a quarter mile south, in the direction of Marietta, then up the other lane and to the other house. I unlocked it and they shivered at how cold it was. The front rooms were empty, but I pointed to the light I kept burning, then led them through to the back rooms which were full of sacks of seed corn, seed lettuce, seed radish, and fertilizer, where another light was burning. I unlocked one of the back doors and took them out through the yard to the kitchen, where I'd had the door cut bigger to let in the big farm machinery. In one corner were gardening tools—shovels, hoes, pick, rake, and so on—which Mantle grabbed up to look at, for fresh dirt, I suspected, in case we'd buried the money somewhere. But Edgren stood in the door looking around. Suddenly he turned to me, saying: "Your father built it, you say. Where was your father from?"

"Texas," I told him.

"That's right, this is a Texas ranchhouse. The dining room's in the house, and they cooked here in this kitchen. But in the old days, the slave boy that carried in the food had to whistle as he came—so he couldn't lick the gravy off the meat. If he didn't whistle, he was in real trouble."

"My father mentioned that."

Edgren seemed satisfied. If Mantle was, I couldn't be sure.

We drove back to the other house, where they were

all getting quite sociable, Mom telling Knight and Bledsoe "how messy his brains looked, scattered all over the ground," the nurse sitting with Jill, and York in the hall talking on the phone. "Nothing," Edgren reported to Knight. "So far, anyway," Mantle said, slightly amending the report. But it was York who took charge of the conversation when he came out, first dropping a bill in Mom's lap and thanking her for letting him use the phone.

"That was Mr. Morgan I was talking to," he explained. "Russ Morgan, I mean, president of Trans-U.S.&C. He's cleared it all up, I think, in regard to the money—as far as Jill is concerned. He's given it to her—in appreciation for what she's done. I suggested the idea to him, and he didn't even let me finish. 'She's got it coming,' he kept saying. 'Oh, brother, has she.' It's hers if it's ever found—and if it's *not* found, she'll still be nicely rewarded. That's one thing about Mr. Morgan. He always does it big. So . . . that winds it up, I think. Jill can't very well be held for stealing money that's already hers."

That got a blank stare.

"Well?" he asked Knight.

"She's not charged, Mr. York."

"OK—but now she can't be."

"Listen, anyone can be!"

"Easy does it."

That was Bledsoe who always wanted to shade things a little bit, "so we don't meet these issues head-on."

No one mentioned holding us, and Knight got up.

"They should do the autopsy tomorrow," he said, "so we'll be holding the inquest Tuesday. All three of you—Mr. Howell, Mrs. Howell, and Miss Kreeger—will be called as witnesses, so please make yourselves available to testify." He put on his coat and started for the door. "We ready?" asked York, turning to Jill.

"I guess so," she told him, half turning to me.

"I'm taking her in," I said, reaching under her knees, as I had quite a few times, putting the other arm around her and lifting her up.

"Well?" she smiled at York. "I don't really have much choice. I have to do what Dave says."

"All right," he said rather grumpily.

Knight nodded to everyone then went out the front door, got in his car, and drove off. "We'll let you know," said Edgren, and he and Mantle left. Bledsoe looked at his watch, gave Jill a little pat, nodded to Mom, and left. The nurse and York left. I turned to Mom and said: "Be back," but whether she heard me or not, I didn't know, as she didn't look at me.

I carried Jill to the door and she opened it. When we were out, she pushed it shut. I carried her to my car which was parked beside the house. I opened the door and helped her climb in.

"Well?" she asked when we'd turned onto route 60, headed for town. "Was I all right?"

"Perfect," I answered. "I was relieved that you left out what was said in the dark, that stuff you thought meant that *she* meant Shaw should kill you. I don't think she did, but—"

"I don't think it—I know it. Don't you know why I left it out?"

"All right, why did you?"

"It was because of you. She's your mother, and I—"

"Yes? You what?" I asked as she stopped suddenly.

"Don't you know?"

"No, I don't."

"Then it's not up to me to tell you."

"Who's it up to, then?"

She didn't answer, but hooked her hand in my arm and whispered: "Are we getting somewhere together or not?"

"So far as *I'm* concerned, we are."

"Then a woman sticks by her guy whether she likes his mother or not. I couldn't talk against her."

"Jill, I love you."

"And I love you."

She leaned back, still hanging onto my arm.

We got to the hospital which looks out on the Muskingum but which also commands a view of the Ohio. I parked the car, but when I reached in for her legs to lift her out, she motioned me off and climbed out of the car herself. She caught my arm, limping a little, but turned to the terrace above the river, took a few steps, and stood there looking at it. Then, chugging through the twilight, we heard an engine laboring. There was the top of a tow, moving up the Ohio, its red light shining at us. It's always a beautiful sight. We stood hand-in-hand looking at it. Then suddenly, in a somewhat different manner, she asked me: "Dave, did York say that money is mine?"

"That's right, if it's ever found. If it's not found, you're to get a reward anyway. So, I just fell in love with an heiress."

"Dave, it's going to be found."

"Listen, Jill, don't hold your breath. If you ask me, that money's in the Muskingum right now, soaking up water to feed the fishes."

"If you ask me, it's not."

She looked up at me with a new glitter in her eye. "That woman, that Mom character, knows where it is and means to keep it. Which mightn't have meant so much to me so long as it was Russ Morgan's. I'd want him to get it back, but mightn't do much about it. Now, though, I intend to do plenty. It's mine and I'm going to get it. I don't know how yet, but I know who knows where it is."

"Mom? How would she know where it is?"

"She knows where she put it, doesn't she?"

"Listen, how *could* she have put it anywhere?"

"By picking it up, throwing it in the boat, and rowing off with it. Dave, it's what that officer thought that was so odd—that Shaw would stand around on that island with me and not say a word about its being gone. And they were right. Dave, he must have had it. He must *still* have had it slung on his shoulder all the time. And she couldn't wait to get out there. That means she took it, unstrapped it from his shoulder and went downriver with it. Or upriver. Or crossriver. Somewhere. Could be, it's on the island. The police didn't search there."

"I told them they could. It's my property. It was part of the farm I bought."

"Well, they didn't."

What that had to do with it, or with anything, I didn't know, but we kept talking about it, and her eyes kept squinching up. Then: "Dave, since Shaw didn't kill me—OK, I could try to forget what she meant because I'm in love with her son. But when it's a hundred thousand dollars, I don't forget anything. She's got it, and I mean to have it. If that puts her in Marysville prison, that's how it has to be. I love you, but if you think I'm giving that money up, I don't love you that much."

"OK, then, now I know."

"I hate to say it, but—"

"You don't love me that much."

Suddenly tears were on her cheeks, glittering under the lights. I said, "Suppose it turns out opposite? Suppose she doesn't have it? Suppose it's never found?"

"*It's going to be!*"

"So you say."

"I want to go inside."

9

———————————

I put the car out back and went in the front door.
The living room was just as it had been, but Mom was
nowhere in sight. I called, but she didn't answer. I
tapped on the door of her room—that is, what had been
the dining room. When there was still no answer, I
opened the door and went in. By then it was nearly 7:00,
almost dark, so I wasn't sure at first whether she was in
there or not. Then I made her out, lying on the bed, still
in the same dress, the blanket half pulled over her, face
up, staring at nothing. I whispered: "What's the big idea,
not answering when I call?"

Still nothing.

"Hey!"

Still nothing.

I took hold of her arm and shook her. She flung it
off and slapped me. I slapped in return, which was where
I made my mistake. She whirled to her knees on the bed,
so the dress ripped open. Then she began beating me
with her fists, in between clawing at my face and
grabbing me, to hold me close and bite me. I didn't yelp

and neither did she. It was grunting, gasping fury, with me fighting her off and her fighting back in. At last she flopped back on the bed and started to bawl, so I could go to my room, to the den, to have a look in the mirror and see what she'd done to my face. It was cut up all right. After slapping the Listerine on, I got the bleeding stopped and finally went back to her. Her crying seemed to have stopped, but as soon as I opened the door, it started up again, the old camp-meeting yodel, loud, clear, hopeless, and 100 percent phoney. I said: "OK, knock it off or I'm letting you have it."

All that got was more of the same, but louder.

I hauled off and slapped her, first on one side of the face, then on the other. She just hollered louder. I got a pitcher of water and started to pour. "Cool it or you're getting cooled."

She didn't quite stop but did ease off, so I knew at last that we could talk. "Now," I asked her, "what's this all about? What in the *hell* is it all about?"

"Oh!" she wailed. "That I should live to see this day!"

"What day?" I wanted to know. "It's Sunday. What other day is it?"

"After all these years, after all I've done, slaving and scrimping and slaving—"

"And don't forget those fingers," I reminded her. "Working them to the bone." Because, of course, I'd heard some of this before, in one connection or another. In fact, I knew most of it by heart. But this time she went on and on, reciting it by the book, leaving nothing out. It wasn't until all of it had been said two or three times that at last she got around to the night before. "And then to think, that when at last there was hope, when the sun was coming up, when the rainbow had showed in the sky, that I should be stabbed in the back—by my own little boy, and a horrible Jezebel!"

"Where was this creature? I didn't see any Jezebel."

"A slut, that slept up with men, then took up with my own little Davey!"

"Hey! Little Davey is me!"

"Just a Jezebel!"

"How you know she slept up with guys?"

"I can tell by looking at her. Anyone can tell. That rotten look on her face."

"And sleeping up with guys, that makes her a Jezebel?"

"What do you think it makes her?"

"I wouldn't know what it makes her—maybe nothing. What she is is a very nice girl."

"I say she's a Jezebel."

"Sleeping up makes her that?"

"What do you think it makes her?" she said again.

"Maybe a girl in love."

"Love? Love?"

"Mom, tell me something."

"Tell you what?"

"There was a girl I looked up, that I had reason to look up. Named Myra Giles, who sounds a lot like you. She was sixteen years old and went in the hospital here to have a child. She had it and two months later got married. So she must have been sleeping up. Does that make her a Jezebel?"

She raised up on one elbow and stared at me a long time. In the dark her eyes looked big, no longer blue, but black. "When did you find that out?"

"Oh, a few months ago. I was getting my papers in order for some insurance I thought I might buy. They want birth certificates, parents' marriage license, and so on. So I went down and looked myself up. It's OK with me. All I saw in those papers was a sixteen-year-old girl who was in love. There's no law against it. I glory in her, and if I'm what came of it, I'm thankful for that, too. But let's get back to the subject. Did that make her a Jezebel?"

"Could be, it did."

"Well, Jezzie, hello."

"How'd you like to go to hell?"

"Well, you said it, I didn't."

"You bet I said it. I have to. But it wasn't me."

"Not you? Are you being funny?"

"It wasn't me, now you know! I wasn't even supposed to tell you, you're not my son! And Jody was not your father! It wasn't me who had you! I was the one who got married, but I didn't have you! It was Big Myra, my cousin who has the same name and went into the hospital there, the clinic they had on Fourth Street. But then, when she couldn't keep it, she begged me to take it and raise it. So to do that I had to get married. We were going to, Jody and I, but we weren't ready to then. But with her nursing that baby, he was so cute. I wanted him. So we went and got married sooner, sooner than we had intended. I love you, I always did, but you're not my child at all, and there's no reason I shouldn't—"

"Shouldn't what?"

70

"Whatever I feel like!"

"Like bellering around?"

"What do you mean by that?"

"I mean Jezebellering."

"You quit talking to me like that!"

"And you quit talking to me like that! That's a hot one, Mom, ain't it? All of a sudden, so you can unzip my pants and take out what's in there, you tell me you're not my mother. Isn't it time to laugh?"

She pushed me out of the way, got up, and turned on the light. Then she stood pulling her dress and twisting it, to straighten out the places where it was ripped or torn or strained. Then she went in the living room where the light was already on and sat down. After a while she said: "If you want to laugh, laugh. I wouldn't know what at."

"At that comical tale you told."

"If it's comical to you, it's comical to you. It never was to me. And it never was to Big Myra."

Why it took so long for it to sink in, to penetrate my mind, that it might be true what she'd said, I don't have any idea. Until then it hadn't occurred to me even to wonder about it. But when she mentioned Big Myra, who I'd always supposed was my aunt, I suddenly had a flash. I saw the look Aunt Myra would have when she'd bring me a toy, a horn or a skateboard or a drum, that always made me so happy. She looked a little like Mom, a shade taller, and slim, but instead of being pretty, beautiful—pale, with blue-black hair and big black mountain eyes. That coloring, they say, comes from Indian blood. She doted on me, and God knows I doted on her—and I knew now the reason both ways. I went

71

over to Mom, put my hand on her head, turned her face to the light, and said: "You're telling me the truth?"

"Yes, of course I am."

"Why didn't you tell me before?"

"It was part of how we fixed it up. I had to promise I'd never tell you, so—"

"So what?"

"You wouldn't mess things up."

"With Aunt Myra, you mean?"

"Her or—anyone."

It must have been five minutes before it dawned on me who she was talking about. "You mean, my father?"

"I mean like I said, with *anyone.*"

"Goddamn it, answer me."

"OK then, with him."

"Who is 'him'?"

"I don't know; she never said."

"Mom, spit it out. Who am I?"

"Don't you think I'd say if I knew? Now that I've said this much? She was working in Logan County, had a job with the Boone County Coal Corporation, a typist or something. And a guy came along who was married. He was taking a survey for a bus line they wanted to run. She never would say who he was, and that's all I know about it."

More time went by while I soaked that up a bit. Then: "Mom, did he have something to do with it, the deal you made about me? Did *he* want you to take me too?"

"I don't know. I never saw him. Maybe he came on, maybe he stayed with her there in Marietta while we were talking about it. She never said. I don't know."

"And why did you take me in?"

"I already said, I loved you."

"And my father, I mean Jody Howell, what did he think about it? Did he love me?"

"At least he loved *me*—then."

"And that's why he agreed?"

"Well, why wouldn't he agree? By then we knew I couldn't have any children. The doctors had already told me."

I already knew she had some kind of condition that made it impossible for her to have children, so I didn't go further with it. More soaking in took place, with her sitting there in her chair, kicking her foot, and now and then looking at me. She had a hunted, guilty expression, not the one she had had when she kept staring at nothing. After some minutes, though, it began to gnaw at me that the whole story hadn't been told. Now I had more flashes, of how my father had acted toward me, the cold way he had. I never felt toward him the way I'd felt toward Mom or toward Aunt Myra. Pretty soon I asked: "What made him so willing? So willing for you to take me?"

"I already said: he loved me."

"Was that all?"

"It was all so long ago. I don't remember."

"Was any money paid?"

"Well, I would imagine so, yes."

"How much?"

"I don't know. It was paid to him."

After a long time I asked, "Was it that that he used to buy the other place with and build that crazy house?"

"I don't know. He didn't say."

"Did he or didn't he?"

"He didn't tell me everything!"

"Was board paid for me?"

"I don't know."

"They wouldn't have paid that to him. They'd have paid it to you."

"Who is 'they'?"

"Aunt Myra and my father."

"Sometimes something was paid."

"Like the first of every month?"

"I don't know; it's been so long."

"How long?"

"What do you mean, how long?"

"Since board for me was paid."

"I said, I don't remember."

"Is board still being paid for me?"

"You quit banging at me."

"In other words, it is?"

She didn't answer, which meant it was, and at last I eased up on her. I had to. By now I'd found out so much that my head was spinning around. I was like a cow that had cropped all the grass it could hold and had to lie down a while so it could chew its cud. I had no idea yet how I felt about it, whether I liked it or not, changing Mom for Aunt Myra or my father for some other guy I knew nothing at all about, except that he must have been decent and really in love with Aunt Myra to put out for me all those years. Also, of course, he must have been able to, which meant he was not just a nobody. All that, though, was stuff that just rattled around. One thing, though, remained to be cleared up. Why, after keeping her pledge all those years, did she up and tell me now? When I asked her, she sidestepped the question. "It had to come out," she whined. "It had to be told sometime."

"Why did you tell me tonight?"

"I don't know, it just came out."

"To make it all right for you to take off your panties for me?"

"How can you say such a thing?"

"Because it's true."

"It's not true! You should be ashamed. You should get down on your knees and beg forgiveness of me."

"I don't. It's true."

"It's not!"

"It is, but get this: It's not going to happen between us. You know why? I don't want it to, that's why. I don't love you that way."

"It's not what I meant, no!"

"It *is* what you meant. Quit lying."

She started to cry, and I went over to wipe her eyes. Letting her blow her nose made me gulp; I wanted to kiss her, and did. That was my mistake. She grabbed my hand and kissed it and then pulled me down in her lap, kissing me and slobbering on me. Pretty soon I wrestled clear and said: "So—now we've gone over it, haven't we? Really talked things out? Know what I want? Something to eat. I'm hungry. How about you?"

"You mean, you're cooking my supper?"

It had an intimate sound, but anything to get to something different from what we'd been talking. "That's right."

"Dave, you're so sweet."

The peas and the salad were part of what had been brought by the neighbors that day. The chicken was from a package of legs already cut, that I'd picked up in market the day before. The pie and ice cream I kept on hand all the time. Whether she took my making her supper as meaning something romantic, that I can't say, but the way she let down her hair, sitting there at the table with the torn dress twisted around seemed to say that she thought I'd changed now that I knew our relation was different from what I'd thought and that I was willing to make a fresh start. That's not how it was with me. All I wanted was something to eat and a change of subject while I thought over all I'd heard. My head wasn't spinning around, but it was turning and turning and turning as I tried to get used to it—that Aunt Myra was really my mother and that some guy who wasn't yet named, some big wheel by the way he'd acted about me, was my father.

She puttered around while I was washing up, grabbing a cloth and wiping the dishes, always taking care to show more than the law allowed. When we went in the living room she tried to sit in my lap. I turned on the TV and got the 11 o'clock news. At last I said I was tired, and how about going to bed? She hemmed and stuttered but at last went to her room after telling me good night.

I went to bed and was at last alone in the dark with what I'd been told. It may seem funny, but little by little things cleared. I found I didn't mind that Aunt Myra was my mother—on account of her big black eyes, the way she doted on me, and the way I doted on her. But the rest of it—who my father might be—was just a great big ache, a hollow place in the dark I had to find out about. I was still thinking about it, or imagined I was anyway, not knowing I'd fallen asleep, when I moved and touched something in the bed. A hand was laid on me and a low whisper came. I must have jumped. "Don't be scared, Dave. It's me, Mom."

I felt around. She was there, beside me under the covers, without a stitch on. I jumped up, or tried to jump up, but she grabbed me and held me close, still whispering: "I don't bite! You don't have to be afraid! Hold me close and love me! It's all right! It's nature!"

"It's not all right. Get out!"

"No! No! Please!"

"Mom, I said get out! No such thing can happen between us!"

"But it can between you and that girl?"

"Leave her out of it, please."

"I won't leave her out of it, no such. We were happy—before she came—just the two of us, talking about how nice we would have it when our little dreams came true. I knew all the time that my secret, the one I told you tonight, would make it all right, what we wanted to do and what you *had* to do! Don't you know that I had caught on to what you were going through? What a man your age goes through? What he needs from a woman? Don't you know that I was willing? To give you all you wanted and more? You wanted it too, from me—oh yes you did. I could tell. Then she had to butt in. I hate her, I hate her, *I hate her!* Why did you take up with her? Why—?"

"I didn't take up with her."

77

"OK, you didn't. So now it's my turn, right now!"

"I tell you, no!"

"Yes, yes. Here, let me—"

I think there was more. The way I remember it, we wrestled and fought a long time, naked there in the blankets, me getting a startled idea of how young she really was, and soft and stacked. Finally I threw her out, out of the bed and out of the room, locking the door, which I should have done in the first place. Then I sat there panting, while she sat in the living room crying. Then it stopped, and I heard her go in her room. I got back in bed and tried to think where that put me. Pretty soon I heard her door open, but easy, an inch at a time, as though she was sneaking through. I braced myself for another session with her, wondering what I would do if she tried to break down the door. Then I heard the rasp of the dial and her voice talking low on the phone.

After a long silence, a hinge squeaked just once—the one on the front door. I heard a step on the porch, then nothing, and finally the sound of the car. Then lights. When I jumped up and looked out, she was driving down to the highway, toward town. Where she was headed, I had no idea and didn't care, even slightly. All I could think of was that now, at least for a while, I was rid of her. I went back to bed and resumed where I'd left off, about this question I had to have answered, this riddle that was now my life: who was I?

10

I may have slept a little, but not much. I kept working on it, putting this, that, and the other together, that I remembered from when I was little and from what I'd been told occasionally. Then it was morning, and I knew I had to talk, to tell it, to let it out, to the one person I wanted to know it, the one person who mattered to me—Jill. I jumped up, went in the living room, and looked Marietta Memorial up in the book. I called and they gave me her room number; then she was on the phone.

"Jill, if you love me, get out here and get out now. Something's happened, and I need you. Take a cab."

"What's your mother going to say?"

"She's not here."

"Oh my! I can't bear it!"

"Jill, hurry it up!"

"OK, soon as I grab me a bite of breakfast and find out who's paying my bill."

"Forget about breakfast. I'll make you some when you get here!"

I guess the next hour, while I stomped around out front, was the longest I'd ever spent in my life. Actually, I couldn't make with the stomping until I'd put in my call to the place where I worked in town, the filling station I mean, to say I couldn't come in, that I had to stay at home in case the deputies came for more questions. I hated doing it. I was in line for manager later on in the summer. My qualification for the job—my main qualification anyway—was that I was steady. I showed up for work every day. I was sober. I got things done. And the customers believed what I said. But as soon as I started explaining the fix I was in, Joe cut in. "Forget it, Dave. My God, it's an honor. The whole town's talking about you. You're in every paper there is, you're the county's number one hero. Take all the time you want."

I went out to think that over and walk around waiting for Jill. At last there was the rental car and then she was getting out, a bundle of newspapers under her arm as thick as a hickory tree. I kissed her and grabbed her to carry her in, but she held off and said she could walk—which she did with a limp but steady enough. She was still in the nurse clothes from the day before, but was due for a whole new outfit, later that day, she said, "from a shop in Marietta that Bob York found in the phone book. And a room in a hotel, a sure-enough hotel, to stay in as long as I'm here. And a thousand dollars cash to 'tide me over.' I'm Jill—fly me. Being a star pays."

By then we were inside, and I folded her in. We stood there a long time holding each other close. Then we opened the papers on the floor. There were a couple from Columbus, one from Akron, one from Pittsburgh, two or three from Chicago, but none from Marietta. The

Times is an evening paper and wasn't due out until later. Sure enough, side by side on page 1 of all the papers, there was Jill and there was me—me in my sheepskin jacket, she in her hospital bed. There were also pictures of Shaw, a small inset blown up from a snapshot and one of Russell Morgan with a pipe, looking important. How that happened, how all the papers had pictures when only three had sent reporters, had been explained by the *Times* reporter. They were wired to the papers. "It's a regular gold mine for us," the reporter said. "Boy, we'll clean up on this—on top of the special we'll send, signed by me, under my personal byline."

After a while we remembered breakfast. I made eggs and fritters. Then at last she asked: "What was it, Dave, that you wanted to tell me?"

"I'll get to it."

"Well? I'm listening."

But for some reason, to tell it that way was tough. I couldn't seem to do it. A little later, though, when we were back on the living room sofa, her head on my shoulder, her hair brushing my nose, I began edging toward it. "Something's come up," I said. "Something Mom told me last night. Or this morning, whenever it was. Before she blew with the car."

"Told you? About what?"

"Who I am."

That was when I knew that what was between us two was a whole lot more than how pretty she was or how we loved each other. She twisted to look at me, then squinched her eyes up, and whispered: "OK, Dave, I'm with it. What is this?"

"She's not my mother."

"I wondered about that."

"How did you catch on?"

"She didn't act like a mother."

"You can say that again."

"What's the rest?"

I told it little by little, going back to Aunt Myra—how beautiful she was, how wonderful she'd been to me, the things that had happened with her, like the time my cart got busted, when one of the wheels came off, and she took it to a garage to get it fixed. But I kept shying away from my father, until she cut in to say: "Dave, you can trust me. Say what's on your mind, what you're leaving out."

"You mean, about *him?*"

"Who is 'him'? Did she say?"

"She swore she doesn't know."

"You believe her?"

"I think if she'd known, she'd have said so. From what she said, he's not from the Big Sandy country. Could be she never heard his name."

"He must be somebody, though."

We talked then, me with that wonderful feeling that I could talk it out with her. Sometimes we'd think of some angle together, like the deal that must have been made for my board and keep and expenses and how my father must have it, have plenty to lay on the line, to make such an arrangement as that, and how much he must love Aunt Myra.

Then she said: "Dave, something's on my mind, my locket. I hadn't expected to mention it, on account of her, her being here, I mean. It would have meant I'd have to come in, and I couldn't have. But now that she's not here—?"

"Your locket, you said?"

"I had it on a chain around my neck when Shaw pulled me out of that plane. It could be out there on the island! If we went out and looked now—?"

"Right away now, quick."

We went down the path to the river, to row out in the johnboat. But when we got to where the boat had been pulled out on the bank, it wasn't there any more. It was half-capsized on a tree, a snag from upriver, between island and bank, that had washed down some years before in the flood that made the island and which moved a few feet each year as a rise would lift it along. There had been a rise in the night, perhaps from Saturday's rain, that had not only moved the tree but also the boat. "That's nice," I said. "You lend someone your boat and they don't even tie it up right."

"How do you get it back?"

"You'll see."

"Dave, don't try to wade in or swim to that boat. You can't. You've no idea how cold that water is."

"Who's swimming? Come on."

We went back to the house and I called Edgren at the sheriff's office. "Sergeant," I told him, "I'm sorry to say that you or your men or somebody did such a careless job of beaching my boat that the river took it away. So it's out in the middle right now, in a place where I can't get it, on a tree trunk, half tipped over. So could you call your friends in DiVola and ask them to get it for me? Come in their cruiser and—"

"OK, no problem."

"The river keeps rising, you know."

"I said OK. Hold everything."

It wasn't over an hour when here came the sound of the outboard and then there the DiVola men were, the same three guys, still in their firemen's helmets. They made quick work of the johnboat, first pulling it clear of the snag, then bailing it out, where it was half-filled with water, and then rowing it in. They were friendly, especially to Jill, it being the first time they had seen her. She told them about the locket, and they offered to help. So we all went out to the island. Then one of them called to her: "Open your hand and close your eyes, I'll give you something to make you wise." So she did, and in her hand he put the locket. She was so happy she cried, and then kissed him to show her thanks. Then the other two said they wanted to be made wise, so she kissed them too. Then we went back to the house for coffee. It was all friendly and warm and wonderful. None of us had any idea of the horrible meaning that boat being hung on a snag had, though.

They left, and Jill and I sat on the living room sofa, whispering, going over it once more, and over and over and over it, this news Mom had come up with, as well as stuff that seemed to apply, that I'd remember and come popping out with, from when I was little and we'd lived in the old house, praying for spring to come when we wouldn't shiver so much. She wanted to go over and see it, but I said we'd better stay there in the new house where we were. People were sure to come for one reason and another, and I'd been asked to stay put.

Sure enough, around noon a bunch did come, people from upriver, with more stuff to eat. It was Ohio friendliness. It started Jill off crying, but then she started eating, which seemed to cure the tears. Then a man named Douglas came. He had the next place upriver. He came over to see how things were, so he said, but the rest of them kidded him about it, saying it was just his excuse to drop by and meet the hero. "And heroine," added Jill, and they all gave her a hand.

They left, and so did Jill, "to pick out some clothes at that shop and be idemnified at the bank so I can draw some cash."

"Identified."

"It's what I said."

"Dave, does this change things at all? Your finding out who she is? That she's your stepmother, instead of your mother?"

"How change things?"

"Do you want me to prosecute?"

"Why would I?"

"Well? She deceived you, didn't she?"

"Listen, that was the deal."

"I was just asking, Dave."

"In spite of last night, if that's what you're talking about, I've thought of her as my mother for years."

"OK."

"If she should be prosecuted, I'd have to help her out."

"OK, *OK*."

11

I sat around for a couple of hours, with more people
dropping by and then leaving pretty soon and the phone
ringing every few minutes. Edgren called to say the
inquest had been postponed from that day to the day
after next. I said: "Just let me know when. I'll be there."

"Will you tell Mrs. Howell?"

"Sure," I told him. Well? I would have if I could
have, and whether I could, he didn't ask me. Some
newspapermen called, especially the one from the
Times, the *Marietta Times* I mean, and I gave them
what little news I had, about the postponement of the
inquest and Jill finding her locket. Jill called to say she'd
moved out of the hospital to a motel in the center of
town, one York had found her, and asked whether she
should call Edgren and tell him. I said that York could
do it, then changed my mind and said she should do it
herself. She said she'd be out in a little while.

I went back to thaw out a lamb roast and check
whether I had mint jelly. I was just about done when she
came, looking so pretty I wanted to cry. She had on a

beautiful winter coat, dark brown, and under that a bottle-green mini that was perfect with her hair, beige pantyhose, and loafers she said were "frumpty," but "are comfortable on my feet." I didn't think they were frumpy, but couldn't rightly say for looking at her legs, which were beautiful. She didn't mind being told, and in fact lifted the mini so I could see all the way. We were in each other's arms when a car drove up.

When I looked, Uncle Sid was getting out. He was Mom's brother, not only mountain but looked it: six feet, thin, raw-boned, and lanky. He had on a dark-blue flannel shirt, gray striped pants, and black windbreaker. But what you noticed most was the hat—black felt, kind of rolled up at the sides and pulled down low in front. It didn't make him look mean, the way a wild kid looks mean; somehow it made him look important. But mostly, he looked like someone you shouldn't monkey with. I let him in and introduced him to Jill. He was polite, but cold. He mentioned that he'd seen her picture and, pointing to the pile of papers still on the floor, explained: "I mean in the papers, miss. That was a terrible thing to be snatched from a plane that way." And then, to me, almost in the same breath: "Where's my sister, Dave? Where's your mother?"

"Uncle Sid, why don't you tell me? It was you she called, wasn't it? Before she left the house? Before she drove off in the car?"

He blinked without answering, and I added: "Well, it was, wasn't it? Where was she headed for? Your place? Flint?" Flint was the village on the Monongahela, where he lived and where she originally came from.

"Well, she might have called me at that," he said finally in that left-handed mountain way that never quite lines it out straight. "I don't say she didn't."

"Then she must have said where she was headed for. Was she headed for Flint, or wasn't she?"

"Flint's her home, Dave."

"Then that's where she figured to go?"

"We could expect her to."

"It's what I want to know."

"But maybe she didn't get there."

"Not yet, you mean, Uncle Sid."

"She should have, by now."

"Give her time."

"Does that hit you funny, Dave? That she should haul out of here, bang, just like that, at three in the morning?"

"It does and did—at the time."

"What made her do it, then?"

"She got sore at me, is all."

"What about?"

He sounded ugly as he said it. I counted three before trying to answer, but while I was doing it, Jill broke in: "Me, I was the what. She didn't like me, Mr. Giles."

"Why not?"

"I'm going to marry David."

"I see . . . I see." Then: "You were here, then? You spent the night with Dave? I don't wonder she kind of got sore."

"No, sir. I was in the hospital."

"But I was here," I said. "She came to my room, screaming. She called Jill a Jezebel and other things too,

88

still worse. One thing led to another, like her trying to beat me up." I showed the tooth marks on my cheek and went on: "Then she slammed back in her room. Later she came out and called you. Finally she went outside and drove off in my car."

"Where to?"

"I don't know."

"Dave, I asked you where to."

"Goddamn it," I roared, going slightly mountain myself, "knock it off with the third degree. I told you, I don't know where to. What's more, I don't much care. Now how'd you like to get the hell out?"

"I'll go when I get ready."

"I'm telling you: go now."

I stood up and went over to him, where he'd sat down on the sofa. He got up and started backing away. I picked up his hat, which he'd put beside him, and handed it over to him. He took it and went, still backing, and not once looking at Jill. "*Well!*" she exclaimed. "Talk about unruly passengers! He was one for the pilot to deal with. . . . And the pilot did!" She gave me a little admiring shake. "I love it, how you deal with them."

"I never liked Uncle Sid much."

We watched as Sid drove off down the lane to the highway. "Do they all dress like that in Flint?" she asked.

"You mean the black hat?"

"He looked like one of the bad guys on TV."

"I hadn't thought of that."

"Well? He did."

"The black hat is pretty much a mountain thing. Yes, they dress like that—at least on Sunday for church. He was all dressed up in your honor."

"The more I see of mountains, the more valleys appeal to me."

"This is a valley, right here."

"The Muskingum Valley— I love it."

"And a mountain is looking at you."

"You're not mountain, at all."

"But I am, as you ought to know."

She put her arms around me, kissed me, then kissed me again. "You mean—it was mountain that sighted that Enfield?"

"Springfield, " I corrected.

"It was an Enfield. I know from my days in summer camp. Our camp mother believed in such things. The Enfield bolt-pull is curved. On the Springfield it's straight."

"You halfway sound mountain yourself."

"David Howell, I've fallen for you—hard, harder than I want. But if you try to make me go mountain, I'll unfall so fast you'll get dizzy. Do I make myself clear?"

I think she expected a laugh, a hug, and a kiss, and they're what I wanted to give her. But all of a sudden I felt a throb in my throat and heard myself ask her: "You want a straight answer to that?"

"I demand a straight answer to it."

"Mountain saved your life."

"All right, all right, all right. Mountain can up and do it, when something has to be done. But don't ask me to take part."

"Don't ask me not to."

We did kiss then, kind of an armistice kiss, but warm and loving at that.

"Tell me more about Sid. What does he do for a living in Flint? What does *anyone* do there?"

"Flint's a dead coal camp of the Ajax Coal Corporation. Nobody lives there but Sid. He's caretaker of the mine and is on the company payroll at five hundred dollars a month and a house, rent-free, that the super used to live in. But that's just the beginning for Sid. His real business is booze which ties in with the mine, and does he make it pay!"

"You mean he mines it?"

"All but. But to understand about that, you must understand a coal mine, especially an abandoned coal mine."

By that time we were on the sofa, with her snuggled tight in my arms. She whispered: "Go on, tell me."

"In the first place, there's the floor which pumpkins up, as they call it, so it's one hump after another. Then there's the top, which first blisters, then falls down on the pumpkins. You can get through, using a miner's lamp, but you have to crawl. So, in through those old dead entries, the worked-out rooms are waiting, just perfect for moonshine stills. Everything's perfect for liquor—the underground spring, running down and into the river, that the mash can be dumped into, so there's no removal problem—the traps, to control the smell—"

"What are traps?"

"In a coal mine they control the air. A trapper boy sits alongside to open it when a train's coming and close it when it goes through. But for Sid they control the smell, which is the main danger a moonshiner faces. Sid can valve it out through the old original drift, where nobody ever goes. On top of that, what deputy would look for a still in that mine? It would be all his life is worth. I mean he'd be terrified. They leave him strictly alone."

"Well, I certainly would."

"And on top of that, there's his help—miners out of work, but before they mined coal, they moonshined. Dust to dust, mountain to mountain, shine to shine. They're doing what comes naturally to them."

"And he's Mrs. Howell's brother?"

"He'd visit her sometime. Like one time he stayed for a week, and I felt something went on, I didn't know what. He came in a car, but going back she had to drive him."

"I don't quite understand."

"What went with his car?"

"Well? What did?"

"I don't know. I never found out."

"Why did the mine close down?"

"Seam feathered out. For 40 years they worked it at seven feet. It was a gold mine made of steam coal. Then it feathered down to four, so it couldn't be worked. But then—how did you guess it?—it could be worked with a strip shovel. On the other side of the mountain, between the top and daylight, it's only 20 feet, so it's crying to be worked, and it is. They put a spur in from the railroad, seven miles up from Flint, called the station Boulder, and are shipping 10 cars a day."

"They say strip mines are bad."

"Not this one. They're smoothing the dirt out again after taking the coal out, planting some in pasture with clover, and putting the rest in trees. To my eye, it looks still better."

"Always the mountain boy."

"OK, I'll drive you over and you can have a look."

"I can't hardly wait."

"Mouth."

"OK."

12

We sat for a long time holding close. Then, around 4:00, she pointed out the window. Another car was turning in from the highway to the lane. It was a Ford, one of the new compacts, and shiny black. It pulled up in front of the house, but when I saw who was getting out, I couldn't help giving a yell. "Who is she?" Jill asked.

"Aunt Myra," I told her.

"Dave, she's beautiful!"

She was, all right, with her big black eyes, pale skin, and soft willowy figure. She had on a mink coat, one I'd never seen, over a dark red dress. Her straight, black hair was combed over her shoulders. She looked like the queen of England, and we stood there gaping at her. Then Jill gave me a push and I went piling out to greet her. I took her in my arms, kissed her, and held her close, and she clung to me. After she'd kissed me two or three times, I took her inside where Jill was waiting to be introduced. But Aunt Myra didn't wait. "Oh I know who you are!" she burst out. "You're the most famous girl in the whole United States. I'm so happy about it!"

At last Aunt Myra asked: "Dave, where's your mother?"

Jill looked at me, and I closed my eyes to think what I wanted to say. Then I knew. "I think right here," I told her.

I went over, knelt by her chair, and kissed her. She broke down and wept on my shoulder, then rubbed her face against mine, so her tears were smeared against me. Then I was crying with her.

"Then Little Myra told you?" she asked.

"Yes, she did."

"When?"

"Last night."

"Why?"

She kept looking at me, wanting more details, but what was I going to say? I hadn't even told Jill all of what had happened, especially that visit to my bed, and I certainly didn't intend to spill it now. "Actually, she didn't mention why, if she had some particular reason. Just that there was something she'd wanted to tell me, something I ought to know."

"Where is she, by the way?"

"I don't know."

"You don't *know*? She moved, is that what you mean? To the other house? Or what?"

"I mean, she left."

"How, left?"

"Just took the car and blew."

"There was a quarrel? Is that it?"

"You could call it that."

"About what?"

I was getting pretty uncomfortable, not doing well at trying to make up stuff, and wanting to knock it off. But once more Jill got in it, with the same answer she'd given Sid. "About me," she snapped.

"Oh—I see."

"She didn't like me much."

Aunt Myra, my mother, sat looking at Jill a long time, and then at last remarked: "That I can well understand." And then, to me: "Dave, Little Myra was getting ideas, or at least I felt she was, that made me very uneasy, ideas that may have accounted for the way she spoke out at last, about me, about herself, and the new relationship she wanted to have with you. Was that her reason? For breaking her pledge at last? Of silence she'd taken to me? In return for what your father did for her?"

"I'd rather not say."

"Then it was?"

She sat there, staring down at the floor. Then after a long time: "I should have come sooner. I've known it was in the wind, that something like this would come. What I didn't know was that it would come this way, with a girl dropping out of the sky."

She went over and touched Jill's hair, and Jill patted her hand. Then she asked me: "What about the police? Or the sheriff's deputies, whoever they are, who have charge of the case? The papers say they told you, and told her, and told Jill, to be available for questioning. What did they say about it? Did they give her permission to leave?"

"I didn't told them about it."

"Has anyone?"

She turned to Jill who said: "I didn't know it this morning when I called from my hospital room to tell them where I was going. They told me all right, come out here, but her name didn't come up."

"Then nobody's told them about it?"

"No, but somebody's going to."

She aimed that at my mother as though expecting approval and maybe a kiss. If so; she got a surprise. My mother's face turned stony and she sat there staring at Jill who suddenly seemed all crossed up. "Miss Howell," she said, "perhaps I ought to explain something Dave hasn't mentioned that's pretty important to me. This woman who he thought until now was his mother has skipped with all my money, my hundred thousand dollars that Russell Morgan gave me, so I couldn't be charged in any way—and as a reward for what I did. If I'm to get it back, she has to be caught. They can't go after her, the police or the sheriff or anyone, until they've been told she's gone. So that's why I have to tell them."

But all that got was more of the same from my mother, a stony stare and no answer at all. After a long time she turned to me, kissed me, and whispered: "I have to be going now."

"What do you want me to call you?"

"What did you call her?"

"Mom—I thought you knew."

"David, call me Mother."

"I'd love to. I want to. Mother." And then, after holding her close: "Mother, who is my father?"

"He'll tell you."

"Yes, but when?"

"As soon as he's free to speak. It won't be long—but don't ask me to say more, David. If I do, I may find myself hoping—and I mustn't, mustn't, ever."

"You mean that someone would die?"

"Yes, that's what I mean."

"And when that happens, what?"

"Your father and I can be married."

"And it's going to be soon, you say?"

"I didn't say! Don't ask me."

"You said it wouldn't be long."

"Then all right, I said that. I didn't say how long is long."

Then at last she turned to Jill and took her face in both hands. She kissed her, then picked up the mink coat, which she had thrown over a chair, put it on, and pulled it around her. Then she opened the door and went out. We both followed, and I put her into her car. She started it, pulled ahead, and swung around the circle in front of the house. As she made the turn, where the circle joined on to the lane, she blew kisses, one to me, one to Jill.

"What did I do?" asked Jill. "I must have done something to change her."

"She didn't change. She blew you a kiss, didn't she?"

"She changed from warm to ice."

"You said you were telling the officers, so they could find Mom."

"Well? Why shouldn't I?"

"OK, but don't ask any help of me."

"Her, we're talking about."

"Or *her*."

"I'm going nuts. Why not?"

"I've tried to explain to you. I'm mountain. She's mountain. Mom's her kin, that's all."

"Didn't you hear what she said? She doesn't respect her."

"You can say that again."

"And yet, on account of this Mom being kin, she'd block me off from making her give back what's mine?"

"I didn't notice any blocking."

"For Christ's sake, I'm going nuts."

"Don't ask her to help."

"Or you to help?"

"I told you, she and I have been close."

"I have to think this over."

She went in the house and sat down off by herself. I sat down and put my arm around her. But she got up, put on her coat, and went out.

13

She was gone for some time. I didn't peep, except to keep track that she hadn't gone off, that her car was still in the driveway. But then I went out to look: she wasn't there. I went around the house, wondering where she could be, and took a chance on the river. Sure enough, there she was. But she hardly turned around when I came. "Dave," she whispered, "it talks."

"You have to be putting me on."

We both kept still to listen. Each time they'd come in clear, the sounds of the river at night, which you don't hear by daylight, how it whispers and burbles and gurgles, and tinkles and tankles and glugs, and sometimes lets go with a roar. She stood drawing deep breaths and listening. "It's beautiful, just beautiful," she murmured. Then she jumped at the sound of a slap. "What was that?" she asked.

"Fish jumping, was all."

"Sounded big."

"Well, why not? Flood time's food time, for him. Plenty to eat, so he grows."

"I never even thought of fish while I was out there—I mean in it. I was, you know."

"Well, they thought of you. They were looking right at you, probably."

"Could we catch one and have him for supper?"

"Why not?"

"Do you have a pole?"

"Handline, good enough."

"Aw, I forgot, we have to have bait, and we can't in the dead of night start digging for worms."

"Aren't shrimp good enough?"

"How do you catch *them?* "

"With a can opener."

"You goof."

We laughed and went up the path to the house. I found the handline in the porch closet and the shrimp in the kitchen. As soon as I'd opened the can, I said: "OK, we're in business, but I warn you right now that fishing's bad for that dress, that beautiful dress Mr. York bought you."

"I'll put on your pants."

"Then OK."

We went in the den where both of us changed our clothes, putting on something rough. We went to the back porch again, picked up the line and bait, and went down again to the river. I showed her how to bait up and said: "You can be the fisherman. I'll row the boat. Now what do you want to catch?"

"Which is the biggest?"

"Carp."

"Then I want me a carp."

"He's big and fat, but the flavor's not too good. He's what's used for gefülte fish."

"Well, 10 million Jews can't be wrong."

"On carp, they could be."

"He's big?"

"Oh, big and fat and thick."

"I want carp."

"Then we'll go where carp is."

I explained that pike and muskalong like it out in the middle, catfish down on the bottom, but carp up in the shallows, "so that's where we'll go after him." On the near side, above my landing, was a creek that had no name, for the reason that it wasn't there except in flood time. But it was flood time now, and I had an idea that carp might like it. So I rowed over, past the snag, past the lower end of the island, and on up to the creek mouth. Jill had never fished before, and I explained what she should do—drop the line overboard, let it run till she felt it touch bottom, then pull it up a few inches, to leave the baited hook above the mud, where the fish would swim to feed. So she reached in the can for a shrimp, baited the hook, and dropped the line overboard. She had hardly pulled it off bottom when she gave a little squeal: "Oh! It twitched! I could feel it! It was a nibble!" But I had her pull in, and of course her hook was bare. We baited the hook and she tried again. Then 10 or 12 feet away, a flash of silver showed, but a big flash, to the sound of a loud flop. "Dave!" she yelped. "One is out there, a great big one. I could see him!" She pulled in, checked that her hook was still baited, and then started swinging it around, I suppose to throw it out where she'd seen the fish. But in mortal terror I crouched down in the boat, yelling, "Don't do that! Stop it! Stop whirling that hook around! Do you want it to rip out my eye?"

She hadn't thought of that.

But the tree saved her the trouble, the one we were pulled in beside, a big white sycamore sticking out of the water just off our bow. Ordinarily it was on land, but with the river in flood, the water had risen around it, so the boat was almost touching it, and the hook, where she'd whirled it around, had snagged in the tree, so we wouldn't be catching fish until we got it out. I told her: "First, sit down. Sit down, keep still, and stop hollering."

She did.

"Now, take hold of me and move from the stern to the bow. *Don't stand up*—or you could go overboard." To trim the boat, I moved from the cross-seat, where I was, to the stern, where she had been. "Now wait till I snug the boat in, jam it against the tree, and hold it tight with the oar."

She did.

I bumped the bow to the tree, then held it tight by shoving an oar to the bottom. The water at that point was no more than two feet deep, so it made as firm a fix as is possible with such a boat.

"Now reach as well as you can without standing up and try to loosen the hook. It has a barb on it, so you may have to twist it. But if you can get your fingers on it, you should be able to get it out."

She reached, but then said: "I have to stand up."

"No! Please! To hell with the hook. Let's go home and have the lamb."

"It's OK. There's a hollow here on the side that I can

hook my fingers into so if I do lose my balance, I can hang on. Hold everything! I can feel the hook, I'm wobbling it. I have it—wind it in."

I did, but she didn't sit down. She said: "I have to shift my position, so I don't go plopping down between the tree and the boat."

"For God's sake, be careful—I can't help you. I have to hang onto this oar so I can steady the boat."

"There's something else in here."

"Probably a hive of bees. Leave it alone."

"It's not bees, it's—"

She handed something to me and asked me to take it, but I dared not let go of the oar, where I had it jammed on bottom, or the boat would veer off and drop her in the water. She said: "It has straps on it and one of them's caught on something. I can't get it loose."

I had a Boy Scout knife in my pocket. I opened it and gave it to her. She tried to take it from me but couldn't hang onto whatever it was she had and stretch far enough to get it. I held onto the oar in the water with one hand, then with the other picked up the second oar, laid it on the cross-seat, put the knife on it, and that way lifted it to her. She took it, cut, and then flung something into the boat. Then she stooped down to the front seat and at last was back in. I said: "Let's go home. Let's look at what you found."

"Yes, I think we better."

We rowed back, beached the boat, then felt our way up the path, and on into the house, both afraid to wonder what we had, yet both hoping. But when we turned the light on we saw what we always knew it would be. There was the red zipper bag, the one Shaw had had, all stuffed out tight, with the end of one strap cut off, where it had caught in some crack inside the hollow. We looked at each other and kissed. Then we pulled the zipper and there the money was, pack after pack of twenties, 100 to the pack, with printed wrappers around them, each reading $2,000. When we felt them, they were damp but not soaking wet.

"Of course," she exclaimed. "The bag went in the river, too, and water would seep in, but only a little bit at a time, through the zipper. It wasn't more than a minute before he climbed out beside me."

"I think we could dry those bills in the oven," and I snapped it on.

But after a moment or two, she said, "Dave, why couldn't we use your plate, that steel thing you have, for cooking fritters? We could heat it, then turn off the heat, put the packs on, and let them stay there and bake. That way, they couldn't burn, but at the same time, we could see what we're doing."

"OK."

So that's how we did it and pretty soon came out with nice new money, all dry, all perfect. "And you know what, Dave?" she whispered. "What the beauty part is? It's all mine! I have the paper to show—Bob York gave it to me."

"That's right," I said. "Wonderful."

"But that's not all."

"Yeah? What else?"

"It's all ours."

"Little Jill, it's yours."

"But what's mine is yours. After all, you're God."

It was beautiful being with her in the kitchen, knowing it had all turned out right and that now we could be happy. She got the paper out of her bag and let me read it. It was in the form of a letter, signed by Russell Morgan, president of Trans-U.S.&C., and listing the bills by number. Then it said something like: "I hereby, as president of Trans-U.S.&C., and by the authority of its directors, do give, assign, and convey the said bills to you, in acknowledgment of your gallantry, bravery, and quick thinking, in saving a valuable plane and the lives of twenty-eight passengers, a pilot, copilot, and stewardess—" I read it, and then she let go of my hand to get up and kiss the money, every pack. I said: "Hey, watch it, you'll blister your mouth."

"You can kiss it and make it well."

"Come here."

She came, and we started being happy all over again. Then she asked: "Dave, what about her?"

"What about who?"

"Well, who do you think? We know who put it there. She has to be the one."

"Then—she put it there."

"Well, what do we do about her?"

"Leave me out."

"What do *I* do about her?"

After a long time, I asked: "Do you have to do anything?"

"OK, but what do I say?"

"In what way, say?"

I knew what she meant, of course. She couldn't just find this money, bank it, and not tell anyone. She would have to tell Mr. Morgan, and from then on the thing would have to come out—in the papers, to Edgren, to Mantle, to everyone. And yet, I couldn't make myself face it. Face up to it, is what I'm trying to say. Because Mom had stolen that money, of that there could be no doubt. And it belonged to Jill, of that there could be no doubt. And Mom had tried to get her killed, of that most of all, there could be no doubt. And yet I was ducking the rap, and I knew why. I was mountain and that's how we do—stand by our kin regardless, no matter how guilty they are.

But over and above that, Mom was still Mom to me, no matter how silly she was or what ideas she'd got in her head. And over and above that was what I couldn't sidestep: she'd stashed that money for me, so we could go off with it, to Florida or some other place, and lay out on the beach with it, and then go inside now and then, to take off our clothes or whatever. Pretty soon Jill asked:

"And what do I *do?*"

When you're backed in a corner, you yell. "OK," I told her, "prosecute. Call Edgren, call Mantle, tell them come out and take it as evidence. Could be a year before you see it again—if you ever see it again. Have you thought of that? Suppose somebody steals it, out of the sheriff's office? Are you sure Washington County is going to be nice about it and pay it back to you, pack for pack and dollar for dollar?"

"You're just saying that."

"OK, *you* say."

"Let's go in the other room."

We started into the living room, but halfway there she stopped and went back to the kitchen. "I can't leave

107

it here," she whispered. "I can't bear to. I have to have it with me."

By then the red bag was dried out or pretty near dried out, and she stuffed the money back in it. Then, carrying it by the two straps she led to the sitting room and sat down on the sofa—still in my pants and jacket. After some time she asked: "You don't want me to prosecute?"

"Well? Would you?"

"Suppose they prosecute anyway."

"You mean Edgren and Mantle?"

"And Knight, if that's his name. That lawyer from the state's attorney's office."

"It's your money, don't forget. If you don't charge her, they can't."

"I'm not so sure of that."

"If it's your money she took—"

"The money's not all."

"What else is there?"

"Her lying to the police—the sheriff, whatever he is, deputy sheriff, if that's it. Giving false information's against the law, and whose money it is is not the whole point."

"So?"

"They could prosecute *you*."

"Me? For what?"

"Yes you, Dave Howell, who looks like God and acts like a mountain outlaw."

"I asked you, for what?"

"Giving false information—giving *no* information, about this Mom character and how she blew. Listen, I have to report this money. I can't let them go on looking for it, trying to find it for me, and not say I already have it."

"OK, then, you have to report it."

"Well, don't I?"

"Listen, it's your money."

"You want *me* prosecuted for lying to them? Not telling the truth is lying, I would think."

"OK, that's what you think."

"What do you think?"

"Do I have to think?"

"I'm going back to town."

"I was hoping you'd spend the night."

"I was hoping to, too."

"I'm telling you right now, if I'd found a hundred grand, the place I'd take it wouldn't be to a Marietta motel, that—"

We sat there, suddenly so self-conscious we couldn't talk or look at each other. Then she went in the den and came out with one of my blankets. "OK," she told me, "I'm spending the night." She put a sofa pillow under her head, stretched out on the sofa, and pulled the blanket over her.

"What's the big idea?" I asked her.

"I'm sleeping here, that's what."

"Oh no, you're not."

I went over and started to pick up the blanket, but a foot drove into my gut. I staggered back against the table. She pulled the blanket on again. "Dave," she said, "good night."

"Good night."

14

Her voice at the phone woke me in the morning. When I looked it was eight o'clock. I went in the living room, and she was just hanging up. "That was Bob York," she told me. "He's so excited he can't talk. He cautioned me, though, not to do anything and especially not to tell anyone until I've talked to a lawyer. Since we already have one, I mean that one who was here yesterday, he thought it was all very simple and would probably 'work itself out,' as he said, without me having to do much of anything—except carry the money to bank. What was that lawyer's name?"

"Bledsoe."

"Will you look up his number for me?"

York had told her to call him at home before he left for his office and not to tip him off over the phone, "what it's all about, because he could easily spread it around without even meaning to if someone is there when you call, before you're together on it about what you're going to do." So she did, but Bledsoe was pretty grumpy about it, telling her call him later at his office, "after I've had a chance to open my mail." So she asked me to talk to him, and I worked on him a little, but think it was my voice, how I sounded over the phone, that alerted him that something big was up. So he said that as soon as he'd had breakfast, he would be out. Her clothes, her regular clothes, the ones she'd changed out of to put on the fishing gear she'd worn during the night, were in my room, and I left her there to dress while I went up and bathed. When I came down she was piling the money on the table in front of the fireplace and folding the blanket over it. We had just finished our bacon and eggs and were back in the living room when Bledsoe's car pulled up. I let him in. He got to it at once: "What is this?" he asked. "But before you tell me, first let me tell you: You don't call an attorney at his home unless it's emergency, and—"

"You don't?" said Jill. "I do."

She stepped to the table and lifted the blanket, and his eyes all but popped out. "My God!" he exclaimed, after he'd stared. *"My God!"*

He sat down in front of it, then looked up and whispered: "You did right to call. I take everything back!"

"There it is," she announced. "Every cent!"

He began counting it, pack by pack. After counting it once, he counted again. "I make it 49 packs," he said. "Where's the other two thousand bucks?"

Now counting it was one thing we hadn't bothered to do, so we did, and it came to what he said, ninety-eight thousand neat, but not the hundred thousand Shaw had baled out with. "So OK," he snapped, pretty sour, "you're shy two grand, and it's not too much trouble to guess where it is. Who stole it, I mean. OK, let's have it. Where did this money come from? *If* you're free to tell me! If not, let's cut it off now, as I don't want to get in a position of knowing stuff I should report. In plain English, then: evidence of a crime."

"That's what's bothering us," she told him very solemnly. "We don't know what to do."

"Are you free to say how you got it?"

"We'll have to say," she said.

"I guess we do," I said when he looked at me.

So she told it. You'd think it would have taken an hour, but it took her about a minute.

Pretty soon he said: "Let me think this over. Let me get alone with it. Let me walk around a few minutes."

He did, circling the house, climbing one of the hills and staring down at the river. I went out to watch, and he called to me to come, so I did. He had me take him up the bank to the boat landing, point out the tree to him, where it stuck out of the water, just up the river, and explain everything that had happened, from our trip in the boat to catch fish to her twirling the hook in the air to her finding the bag in the hollow. Then he led on back to the house where he led in to the living room, sat down, and began: "Well—you have it, there's no getting around that. Possession is nine-tenths of the law. You have that on your side. Nevertheless, in this case the question arises: Can you keep it?"

"Can *she* keep it," I corrected.

"That's it: Can she?"

"Why can't she? Or couldn't she?"

"I don't exactly know, but I feel her claim is quite shaky, in spite of that deed Mr. Morgan drew. It makes the money hers, but it wasn't hers at the time it was hidden. At the time it was hidden—by whom? Do you know?"

"I'd rather not say," I told him.

"Then count me out," he snapped, annoyed. "You're skating on thin ice. I can't be of any help if you make me skate wearing blinders."

He got up to go, but Jill put her arms around him and pushed him back in his seat. "By his supposed-to-be mother," she said.

"Who?"

"You met her. The woman he thought was his mother, except it turned out that she wasn't. She's his foster mother. We assume she hid the money and skipped."

"It certainly looks that way."

He asked some questions, then: "And she's not friendly?"

"Friendly? She hates my guts."

"Well, you can't exactly blame her."

"If you're talking about Dave," she told him very quick, "I do like him, but don't jump to conclusions, please. I did call you from here and did spend the night—but right on that very same sofa, and the reason was money, not romance. I was afraid to take it to town with me, to bring it to that hotel, where it could be stolen, quite easy. It wasn't what you think."

"How do you know what I think?"

"I don't want you to get a false impression."

"I don't think, I know—that you told her to her face she tried to get Shaw to kill you. If you think that arouses love for you, I don't."

113

"I see what you mean."

"But that's not what you told the officers."

"That's right. You told us to take it easy."

"I would say the same thing now."

"Well, what are you getting at?"

"I'm not sure. I have to think."

He took us over it step by step and minute by minute—what had happened out there that morning, what Shaw had said, what I had said, what Mom had said, what Jill had said, and what we all four had done. He took us inside, to my bed, to the bathtub, and Jill lined it out, exactly what had happened, even to my looking like God. When we got done, he got up and walked around with it for quite some little time.

Then: "Your trouble," he said at last, "is that *your* finding the money, conveniently on purpose now, is going to look very suspicious—at least to Edgren and Mantle, who've been suspicious from the start. You can say all you please, that you found it completely by accident while trying to catch a carp, but that won't convince these officers, at least, if I know them. And on top of that, if this woman is ever located and vents her spite on Miss Kreeger by saying you all three did it, then you're really in trouble."

"Why?" asked Jill. "The money's mine. What difference does it make what she says?"

"On account of Mr. Morgan. If, from what she says, he gets the idea that the three of you conspired, you and Dave and this woman, to gyp him out of this money, then he can allege that you obtained your deed through fraud and have it declared void."

She flared at that. "Mr. Morgan wouldn't think any such thing."

114

"For a hundred thousand bucks, I wouldn't trust anyone."

That kind of took care of that, but I felt he'd come up with something, and asked him: "OK, get to it. So what?"

"So if you put that money back, in the tree, right where you found it, and then tonight saw a prowler, someone in a boat. If you reported that to Edgren, he'd have to investigate. Then *he* would find the money. Then *no* one could say you knew it was there. This woman can scream her head off, and still you're in the clear. *And*, if you graciously mention reward, a small percentage to Edgren, I don't know how he'd feel—whether he'd take it, that is, whether he'd feel that he could. But he might—just might persuade himself it would be all right—in which case that brings down the curtain. The rest of the money's yours, with no more nonsense about it."

"What do you think?" she asked me.

"Well," I told her. "It's why we got Mr. Bledsoe in it, why *you* did, why you asked him to come out. It covers everything that we were worried about and in a very simple way. At last we'd be playing it safe."

"How much reward?" she asked.

"Well, that's up to you. I would say maybe five percent, which you could well afford. It's off your taxes anyway."

"My—what?"

"You'll pay heavy tax on this 98. On 93 you'd pay less."

"You mean, give him five thousand?"

"Well? For finding your money, for deciding no charges are called for—?"

She sat there staring at him, and then: "I don't know. I don't know what to say. I have the money now. If I put it out there again—?"

"For one night only, remember."

"Yes, but just the same—?"

He sat there a minute but then jumped up to face us. "Wait a minute, wait a minute!" he growled, very excited. "At last I've caught up with this, to know why my instinct told me you have to put it back, that money, in the tree, to let Edgren find it. That woman—it lies in her power, not only to say the three of you hid the money, but that one of you killed him for it—Shaw, I'm talking about. Howell, that one is you. Now if you want to spend the next 20 years in prison while she gets immunity for singing—"

"OK, Mr. Pledsoe, you've said it."

That was me. She sat staring at him.

15

Bledsoe left, and I went outside with him, but she still sat there staring at the money. As he got in his car he said: "I don't think that girl's going to do it. I think she's hipped on that money. OK, it's a lot, and putting it out in a sycamore tree, if only for one night, is a heartbreak——but nothing like the heartbreak it's going to be if it's taken from her and on top of that, she does a stretch in Marysville. She seems to like you, and I think it would help if you remind her that Mrs. Howell holds the cards, if she wants to play them. She's not in your power, as this girl seems to think. She and you are in hers, but bad. Because if you killed Shaw to save a girl from being killed, that's one thing, and no one could possibly mind. But if you killed him to steal the money, if the three of you had that idea, that's a whole new ball game. Unfortunately, it's Edgren's idea, and Mantle's, or seems to be. Police have that kind of mind."

He drove off after calling through the window: "You're still riding for free—no charge for this, Dave." I waved, but when I went back inside, she was still sitting there, still staring at the money. I asked: "Are you going to do what he said?"

"Yeah, it was easy for him to say, it cost him nothing to say it. It's not his money, it's mine. It's mine and I've got it, so why should I give it up? Go hiding it out in some sycamore tree? And another thing: How do I know that Edgren will give it to me? Or that *he* won't swipe it from me?"

"You have to trust someone."

"For one hundred thousand bucks, this lawyer wouldn't trust anyone. Why should I?"

"In other words, you're not going to?"

"I have to think about it."

"Then I have to warn her."

"Warn who?"

"Warn who do you think?"

"Then if that's how you feel about her, and how you feel about me—!"

"Her? And you? What about me?"

"What do you have to do with it?"

"Didn't you hear what he said? So long as she sticks around, she can send the both of us to prison. I'd rather get her out of the way—*try* to get her out of the way."

"And how are you going to do that?"

"I assume she's in Flint—laying low till things blow over and it's safe to pick up the money. I'm going to tell her it's been found, and she'd better make tracks for Cuba. Or Mexico. Or someplace. She may do it. I don't know."

"With my two thousand bucks?"

"It's worth it."

"To whom?"

"Didn't you hear him? To us."

"Of my money, you mean."

"I'm getting a bit sick of your money."

"I'm not."

We sulked at each other, and then she asked: "And how are you going to Flint? She has your car, don't forget. And you're not taking mine, I promise you."

"Truck."

"What truck?"

"Pickup truck I have to haul stuff into town. Out in the wagon shed. What *was* the wagon shed, when it was built."

"Then OK, warn her."

"I'm going to. But I'm also going to warn you. What you do today is going to affect the rest of your life—to make it, financially at least, or wreck it, in every way there is. I strongly suggest to you that you not drive off with this money in your car or carry it to your hotel, or anywhere. And I also suggest that you not do anything before talking to someone else—someone you have confidence in, like York. Be sure you tell him what Mr. Bledsoe said, and once you have his reaction you can take it from there. Now if you'll excuse me—"

I started for the door. She jumped up at last. "Is that all you have to say?"

"I've said too much already."

"Nobody minds, that I notice."

Suddenly I went over and took her in my arms. But she didn't really come to me. After a moment or two she lifted her face and I kissed her. If she kissed back, I can't be sure, but if she did it wasn't a real honest kiss, kind of a halfway thing that said of course she liked me, but at the same time I must remember that one hundred grand was one hundred grand, or that $98,000 was $98,000. It was the kind of a kiss that can count.

Flint was 60 miles, an hour by the old way of driving, an hour and a half now, and it was a beautiful morning, a spring day in March. The first few miles were low hills, rolling country covered with farms, but coming in toward the Monongahela River, the mountains began to show gray, a little cloudy on top as though they were made of smoke and you could throw a rock through them if you could throw a rock that far. At Clarksburg I hit the west branch of the river, and pulled out on a roadside park, to sit and look for a minute and drink it in. I knew then, of course, if I'd ever forgotten it, that I was mountain, and that this country spoke to me, in a way no other country could.

I also wanted to think, to pull my wits together and decide what I wanted to say, face to face once more with Mom. If I played it the way she wanted, it would be duck soup, as I knew, regardless of what had been said or done or not done that night in my bed back home. If I played it a different way, the way I more or less had to, I could be heading for trouble, real trouble, mean trouble. The question was, could I shade it the least little bit, act friendly without starting something I couldn't stop? What I came up with was: take it as it comes; don't cook it up in advance, let her lead to me, don't go out to meet trouble. After a couple of nice inhales, I started up again and drove on, came to Deer Creek soon and followed it up to Flint. I don't know if you've seen an abandoned coal camp, but I do know that if you have, you don't care to see it twice.

At the bottom, of course, was the "creek," a freshwater mountain stream, quite pretty if that was all. Above it was what was left of the spur, the railroad connection that ran down to the main line beside the river. But for whole stretches the rails were gone, with nothing left but weeds. Then when some rails would show they were rusty and slewed around. Above the spur was the road I was driving on that wasn't much but was in better shape than the spur. Above the road were the houses the miners had lived in, all falling apart now, with busted windows and doors hanging off their hinges. But in between were gaps, where houses had been carted off, and those houses had been loaded on trucks and stolen.

When that merry larceny stopped was when Sid Giles got the job of being caretaker and watchman. You didn't steal any house with Sid walking guard in the night. Whether he stole the houses himself, as a way of promoting the job, or had it done, or what, I don't know, but there could have been a connection. Anyway, right now he lived in the "big house," as it was called, the old super's mansion, which was next up on the slope. It was painted a cream color and was really something to see. As I passed I saw Sid's housekeeper, a woman named Nellie, come out and shake a rug. I didn't stop, but took note that my car wasn't there. On account of the rise of the hill, the place had no garage, but it did have a carport, and a school bus was parked there.

Highest of all was the tipple. A tipple is a conveyer belt, a bucket chain that runs down the mountain side from the drift mouth to the spur, and carries the coal down to the railroad gonds. A "drift" is the main tunnel into the mine. From it run "entries," branch tunnels to the rooms where the coal is mined. The mine trains are hauled out by electric locomotives onto a trestle above the conveyer belt. The mine cars dump the coal on the buckets, and the buckets carry it down. In the morning the miners walk up the buckets to the drift mouth, to ride into work on the mine cars, and in winter, of course, it's dark. That is, most of the miners walk up the buckets, but some of them walk up the mountain side by a path. "They look like a long glowworm," a miner told me once, "walking along with their miners' lamps lit. Know who those miners are? They're the one-legged men who lost a leg in the mine. When a miner gets hurt that's *how* he gets hurt—he's 'rolled agin the rib,' as they call it, so it crushes his leg. And after he gets well, the company gives him a job on account they're kind and considerate, and doesn't arrest him for carelessness. There's 20 or 30 of them working in every mine."

The tipple, of course, was falling apart, with the bucket chain all gone, either moved to some other mine or sold for scrap or something, and the housing over it gone. But the trestle was still there, with a straight drop to the road. I wanted to stop and check if what I had heard was true, that Sid had a falls rigged there to lower the booze to his truck for transportation to Fairmont. But stopping was not recommended. It wasn't possible that the place wasn't guarded by thin guys with rifles. You wouldn't see them, but they'd be there.

So I went on to the place I was headed for, which was a cabin back from the road, about a mile above

Flint, in a kind of flat place by a hollow that had been cleared years before for farming and now was used to grow truck. It had a dirt lane leading in, kind of bumpy but not too bad, and was built of heavy logs with two sides hewn off flat and the ends shaped to criss-cross. They were cut short on one side of the house, to let in a stone fireplace and stone chimney rising up. Inside it had two rooms, the one at back with an oil cook stove at one side, a bunk on the other, and table with chairs in the middle, the one in front, with fireplace, settees, and low table. The furniture was old, homemade, and goodlooking, the rugs hooked and beautiful. Even the floor was something to see, being of white pine, scoured with sand until it shone like satin..

Aunt Jane lived there, the head of the Giles family in that part of Harrison County. She lived with Borden Giles, a son, who I knew wasn't home, as no car was there, and so she opened for me herself—a gray-haired woman of 60 but smallish and not bad looking. She had a touch of Mom's slick shape and of my mother's high-toned way of holding herself. She knew me at once—though it was some years since I'd been there—and was really surprised to see me, not just make-out surprised, a point which I noted at once, as she wouldn't have been if Mom was somewhere around. She didn't kiss me, as by her lights she shouldn't, but did shake hands very friendly, first wiping her hands on her apron. It was gingham and clean. Her dress was wool, of some dark color like brown, and under it she had on pants. I patted her hand after shaking it and watched her eyes, how they looked. Sure enough, they were searching my face, trying to guess what I wanted, which reinforced my first feeling that she had no news of Mom or any idea where she was.

She brought me in, sat me down by the fireplace, which had three logs already burning, disappeared into the kitchen, and was gone a couple of minutes. When she came out she had a cup and saucer in one hand, a coffee pot in the other. She poured, telling me: "You see I remember you take it black."

"Thanks, Aunt Jane."

Then, shooting it quick, on purpose, to catch me off balance: "Dave, where's Little Myra?"

"Why do you ask?"

From mountain people, me included, you never quite get a straight answer. They don't mean to deceive you, but they never come right out and say it. "It's what you've come about, ain't it?"

"It might be at that."

"She don't stay with me no more when she comes. Now she stays with Sid."

"You mean, I should go there and ask? Not that I want to."

"If she was there, I'd have heard." And then: "Dave, there's no need for you to go there, and I wouldn't if I was you."

"Aunt Jane, I don't like him."

"I didn't say he likes you."

"Maybe I found that out."

"You mean you've seen him?"

"He might have been by, yes."

"When, Dave?"

"Day before yesterday, maybe."

"Asking for her, was that it?"

"Could have been, at that."

"And she wasn't there, Dave?"

"Not as I recollect."

"He was looking for her, and you are. Where is she?"

"Wouldn't say if I knew."

After a long time: "Dave did she take that money?"

"Oh, so you know about that?"

"I got a TV in the back room. The man on it suspicions her."

"Not on my TV."

"We get Pittsburgh here."

"And they say she took the money?"

"They don't say it, they think it."

"Are you sure?"

"I can tell."

She was right on top of the truth, though not yet the whole truth, and I had to make up my mind about it, if I was going to tell her that Jill had found the money and that that proved that the Pittsburgh suspicions were true. I decided against it. I couldn't control what she'd tell in case Mom showed up and I had Jill to consider in light of what Bledsoe had said—and myself to consider too. Suddenly she asked: "What did you come to tell her?"

"To skip."

"Where to?"

"Mexico, I would think. Anywhere, so it's not in the U.S."

"Get out of the country, you mean?"

"That's it, but fast."

"Dip into that money and—?"

"She ought to have enough."

It had been bothering me that I'd driven straight

over, without stopping for cash at the bank, to fix her up with what it took to skip with. But if she still had the $2,000, as she must have, that she took from the hundred thousand before hiding it, she didn't need any cash from me.

I could feel Aunt Jane's eyes searching my face and knew she must know I was holding something back, but before she could start working me over again, there was the sound of a car outside and then there was my mother—my real mother—parking behind my truck and getting out of her car. I went out to meet her, then helped her out and kissed her. She kissed me and whispered: "Is she here? Mom?"

"No."

She kissed me again and then turned to Aunt Jane, who by then was at the door and who seemed glad to see her. She asked: "Aunt Jane, is Little Myra here?"

"Not that I know of, no."

"Have you seen her?"

"Not as I recollect."

We went inside, where Aunt Jane sat us down, and my mother turned to me. "I haven't seen her," I said.

"I came to warn her."

"Of what?" asked Aunt Jane.

"Of that girl," my mother told her. "Of that Jill, who's on her tail." For a moment, I thought she must know about Jill's finding the money, which I didn't want Aunt Jane told. But then I realized she meant the previous day's conversation, when Jill shot her mouth off so loud. I cut in: "I've just asked Aunt Jane to tell her to skip if she comes."

"What *I* came to say," said my mother.

"And she has what it takes to skip with," growled Aunt Jane, in a tone not friendly to Mom.

We sat back then and visited, with Aunt Jane bringing more coffee and my mother asking about people, all sorts of Gileses apparently, that I'd never even heard of. But pretty soon she got up, and I got up of course. We both shook hands with Aunt Jane, left our greetings to Borden, and went outside. I kissed my mother and put her in, telling her: "Be better if you let me pull out first." As to why it would be better, I hadn't quite figured out, but she said "OK" real quick, as the main thing was not to wink or do anything that might tip Aunt Jane we had stuff to tell each other that we didn't mean to tell *her*. So I patted Aunt Jane once more, then got in the truck and drove off. But I drove slow to make sure my mother was back there, tailing me. As I turned into the road, I kept motioning with my hand, my left hand that is, that she should stay there, behind, and not make any effort to pass. I watched in the mirror, and sure enough her hand gave a little shake, and I knew she understood. It gave me a real lift, that she should know what I meant just from one little wigwag.

16

We drove on, back through Clarksburg, then turning into route 50 and keeping on for some miles, she following right along, till ahead of us was a lookout, one of those parks with a view. I signaled, then pulled out and stopped. She pulled up right beside me, and when I got out we looked at each other and laughed. I think it sent her too, that we'd do things together that way, each one always knowing what the other one meant. I walked to her window and told her: "Something's happened I couldn't tell you back there."

"OK, but first: did you tell her, or did anyone, what Little Myra told you? About us, I mean?"

"No—I couldn't tell just a little bit."

"Of course she knows—but you knowing the ins and out of why—it could have got pretty complicated."

"That's why I said nothing about it."

"So—what's happened?"

"Jill found the money."

"That Shaw had?"

"That's right—all but two thousand dollars. By accident, last night."

I told her about the fishing trip, and her face screwed up in pain, and even when it unscrewed, she sat there with her eyes shut. Then: "That makes it certain, doesn't it? About Little Myra? That she did steal that poke. What now? *What* now?"

"There's more." I told her about Bledsoe and what he had said, and Jill, and what *she* had said. After a moment she said: "I don't blame her, Dave. It's just a bit crazy, that's what, a real lawyer's idea. So don't blame her too much."

"Bledsoe was thinking of me."

"As I am, of course. And Myra, from what you've said, now hates you and hates that girl, with that old time religion of hers that she's full of and that for some reason makes her onery. She's a real danger, but playing it tricky is worse. Jill has the right instinct, Dave."

"I'm not so sure I agree."

"Suppose you did it that way, as this lawyer suggested to you, and the police didn't bite?"

"How do you mean, didn't bite?"

"Didn't fall into your trap? Didn't search the tree?"

"They'd more or less have to, wouldn't they?"

"People never have to do what you want them to do. So they do search the tree, but not until working you over, so they're good and sure and certain you know more than you're telling. Then it's all bound to come out, from the flop of the carp to the lawyer's idea—his not very bright idea. Then it could really mean trouble."

"You're on her side, then?"

"When it's money, hang onto it."

"How about when it's a neck?"

"I'm not so sure it is."

"Well, I'm damned sure that it could be my neck, for instance, and hanging, in connection with it, is not a subject I like to hear brought up—or a stretch in prison, either."

"Dave, there's an angle, a real possibility that's occurred to me since you told me about this, that would make Jill so right it makes me shiver. Haven't you thought of it too?"

"What are you talking about?"

"If you haven't guessed, I certainly won't tell you. But maybe Jill has, and if she has, it makes it all different, the way she's acting about it. And, of course, makes it all different for *me*."

"What in the hell are you talking about?"

"Have dinner with me tonight, and by the time dessert is served, I'm pretty sure you'll guess."

"I have to get back to Jill."

"If she's still there."

"If not, I'll have to call her."

"Will you call me too? I'm at the Two Rivers, that new place down near the armory."

"I'll keep you posted, of course."

What she meant, I couldn't imagine, but it turned out she meant plenty and that what she meant was right—as I found out the next day.

It was nearly 4:00. I got in the truck and drove on. She tailed along for a while, but then at a light I lost her and didn't slow down for her to catch up. It was late afternoon, around 6:00, when I turned into my lane, and my heart gave a great big bump when I saw Jill's rental car still there. I drove around to put the truck in the wagon shed. As I closed the door she came running out of the house, dressed in my pants, one of my flannel shirts, and a corduroy jacket I had. She ran into my arms, kissed me, and whispered: "I'm so glad, so glad. I was afraid you weren't coming, Dave."

"Why wouldn't I come? You're here and I live here."

"You wouldn't if arrested."

"That's an idea, it sure is."

"Stop sulking and kiss me."

I kissed her, but couldn't help making a crack: "If you can interrupt kissing that money."

She pulled back, and slapped me, then kissed me some more. Then: "That's a surprise I have for you, Dave. I have stopped kissing it. I put it back, as that lawyer said." She motioned at her costume, as though it explained everything, but I didn't connect. I asked: "Back? You mean in the tree?"

"Just like he said."

"But how could you handle that boat? You *couldn't* handle it, Jill, rowing upriver in the Muskingum River current!"

"I didn't say I did."

"The left-handed way you talk, you sound mountain already. Come on, say it: What did you do, fly?"

She seemed delighted at my being so crossed up, kissed me once more, then said: "Let's go inside." So we went in the kitchen, and there on the table was ham, two pieces, sliced real thick, fresh peas, shelled in a bowl, potatoes, peeled and sliced shoestring, in a bowl of water, and salami, sliced thin and wrapped in wax paper.

131

She said: "There's our dinner, that you're cooking for us. We're having sliced ham, green peas—"

"I see what we're having," I said. "Get going on what you did."

"Let's go in and sit down."

She took my hand and led me to the sitting room, then sat down with me on the sofa. "Give," I told her.

"Kiss."

I kissed her.

"So," she went on, "you left."

"I went over to Flint to warn her, as I told you I meant to do. No soap. No one over there has seen her or knows where she is. My mother showed up too, in the middle of my call on my aunt, with the same idea I had. So we left, and on the road coming back I told her, what little there was to tell. That's all I have to tell. Now—?"

"I have a great deal to tell. First, I did what you said, talked to someone I have confidence in—as I thought. I called up Bob York at his motel, and sure enough here he came out. Now we have two rental cars. When he heard what that lawyer said, he simply hit the roof—said I'd do no such wacky stuff. But when I reminded him that Mr. Bledsoe was local, that he was a lawyer in touch, he wouldn't even listen—said Trans-U.S.&C. needed no hick advice. We were playing it straight with no funny tricks. That's when I cut in to tell him that we weren't playing at all, that I was playing, and that all I wanted of him was to tell me what he thought. So his answer to that was to call Russ Morgan direct. He put 10 dollars under the phone, and I wasn't able to stop him. So Mr. Morgan and I had to talk. I explained it to him, that if the police didn't believe we found that money by accident while trying to catch a carp, we were right under the guns of that woman who could say we killed Shaw on purpose, out on the island, and then hid the money, and so on and so on till I was going up the wall, but at last he saw what I meant and told Bob York to lay off. So Bob got sore and stomped off and left in his car. But that was just the beginning. Next off, Edgren was out, wanting to know where you were, where Mrs. Howell was, and I don't know what-all. I told him you'd gone to find her and would call him when you got back. Incidentally, I think you'd better."

So we interrupted the conversation while I called the sheriff's office. Edgren wasn't there, but I left word for him that I was back. Then back to Jill. "OK," she said, "but enduring all that talk, little by little, I knew who it was that I loved, and —"

That called for another interruption, with me holding her close, the both of us mingling breath, but no unbuttoning of any kind. Then she went on: "All of a sudden I knew I was going to do it, put the money back—and right away quick, before anyone else came."

"But how?"

"That was it. I couldn't handle that boat, but then I thought of a way. I changed to your clothes, these I have on. I got the galoshes out of the car. The woman in the store insisted I take them 'on account it can rain in Ohio, and when it does it don't sprinkle, but comes down cats and dogs.' That's what she said, and I put them in the car, in the glove compartment. So I went outside and got them, then put them under one arm, wrapped in a kitchen towel, the money being under the other, and hied me up to the landing."

"My landing, you mean."

"Yes, up below the inlet that the tree is sticking out of. So then I sat down, and took off my shoes and stockings, took off your pants and my panties, and then was the cutest thing in Ohio, with a bare bottom Trans-U.S.&C. should put in their ads, it was so pretty. So then I pulled on the galoshes and was ready. I took that money and tramped up to the inlet, then I waded in. Oh, was that water cold. But at least, I could see what I was doing—and went splashing on. By the time I got to the tree the water was up to my bottom, but I dropped the bag in and splashed back. When I got back to the landing I took the galoshes off, dumped the water out, and grabbed up the towel—the reason I had brought it. I wiped myself off quick, then pulled on your pants, my shoes and stockings, the galoshes, and scooted back, thinking how much I loved you. So, how much do you love me?"

I folded her in and told her but once more without any unbuttoning. I admit, I was quite overcome. But when I suggested we prove our love, she said no, we'd better not. "Someone might come, and that would ruin everything. Some damned newspaperman, if he put that in his paper, could ruin everything for us. Better you make dinner now, so we can eat it and then take our time figuring what we say—I mean the story we tell Edgren or whoever answers the phone, that'll get them started tomorrow, to go up there, find the money, and then take it from there."

"OK. Just the same, I love you. Do you love me at all?"

"What do you think?"

17

So I made dinner, frying the ham but boiling the potatoes and mashing them so as not to have too much fried stuff, boiling the peas and cutting two pieces of pie. Then we ate and I washed up. We went into the living room. By then it was eight o'clock, and we sat on the sofa, whispering about what we would do to finish up Bledsoe's idea, which was half carried out already. I think that was the happiest time I'd had with her, up until then, whispering there in the dark, as first I'd think of something and she'd think of something also to make it better. Like when I said I'd gone out before going to bed, "to have a look around, and heard this boat rowing up. When it headed in for the tree I yelled, and it turned and headed downriver"—and she suddenly interrupted:

"Dave, that sounds kind of phoney. *Who* goes out to have a look around? It's something you wouldn't do. But if we *both* went out, not to have any look, but to take a walk by the river and hold hands and watch for shooting stars—?"

"OK, that's how it was."

"And then when this boat came along, we were up on the landing by then, sitting there side by side, *that's* when it came along—"

"Rowing upstream?"

"Yes, past the island, and—"

"On past the landing—"

"And Dave, that's when we held still, as we didn't want to be seen, and—"

"Thought nothing of the boat—"

"That's right, until I screamed—"

"A real Jill Kreeger screech—"

"As it stopped, then headed for the inlet, and pulled up under that tree—"

"Wait a minute—how did we know *where* it pulled up? In the dark? It's 50 yards from the landing up to that inlet, and—"

"The tree is white, Dave—all sycamores are white. We could see the boat against it—"

"So OK, you screamed, and then what?"

"I kept screaming, I did."

"And what did I do, Jill?"

"You hollered at him, that's what. You hollered: 'Who are you, what do you want? What are you doing there?'"

"And you kept on with your screaming. And then?"

"He left, all of a sudden."

"How?"

"He began to row backwards."

"Backing water, you mean?"

"Whatever it's called, Dave."

After some time I asked: "How long did he stay by the tree?"

"No more than a couple of seconds, I would think, Dave. Long enough to get us excited. Not long enough to fish up our money."

"Your money, Jill."

When we had that all straightened out, we got on to the rest of it, my call to the sheriff's office and what I would say. But there we hit a snag, as we were blocked off from me reporting a theft or someone attempting a theft, as to do that I'd have to let on I knew what was in the tree. Then she hit on the idea that I didn't have any idea why someone would come messing around it, but it was on my place just the same, and for whatever reason he had, there somebody was, "and you want protection, Dave. That's what's on your mind. Here they've taken your rifle away, as everyone knows by now, as that was on TV, so everyone out here knows. And you have me to think of—"

"I want them to send somebody out?"

"That's it, Dave—the whole thing's got you scared, and you don't bring up the tree and what might be in it till tomorrow, and maybe not even then. Because whoever comes out, maybe he brings it up. Looks like he might, at that. But what you want is protection."

"In other words, one thing at a time."

"That's right—keep it simple."

"When should I call, Jill?"

"You should call right away quick, after seeing that boat. And people take walks in the early evening, not in the middle of the night."

"In other words, *now.*"

"Dave, I would."

So I called. How much the night clerk cared was exactly not at all. He said the river was public, that anyone had the right to row on it day or night, that no charge could be brought or any arrest made, that the sheriff had no power to act. I said the tree was on my property, and he asked what charge I wanted brought. At that I blew my top. I bellowed into the phone: "So OK, now we know: A girl saves a plane and 28 lives besides the lives of the crew. I save the girl by shooting the guy that was swearing to kill her, and my stepmother tries to save the money the guy baled out with—and the thanks I get is to be told to stand by in case charged—with what, will you tell me that? And on top of that, you take my rifle in and now when I'm completely defenseless, how you help me out is give me a bunch of chatter about the river and how public it is. In God's name, what do I pay my taxes for? A lot of talk from a night clerk? A lot of—"

"Hold on, hold on."

"I won't hold on. I want action, and I mean to get it. Are you sending somebody out or—"

"What's your number, Mr. Howell?"

I calmed down and gave him my number. He said he'd call me back. As I hung up she burst out laughing and I had to join in. Then we were in each other's arms, the tears running down our faces, from how funny it was, and I had a hard time stiffening up, fighting the cackles back, so I could take the call back when it came. He said "An officer will be out. It'll be a half-hour or so; he has to get dressed. If he's to spend the night, is there some place he can lie down?" I said, "Yes, sure," and he said: "OK."

I licked her tears away, the both of us giggling about it, and she said: "I ought to stay, I would think, to put in my two cents' worth. But I have to get dressed. My clothes are in your room."

So we went in there, but before she could dress, she had to undress, and of course I had to help her. So pretty soon she was naked, the second time I'd seen her that way, and it was marvelous to sit on the bed, pull her over to me, and kiss her in all sorts of beautiful places. She didn't seem to mind, and in fact helped once or twice, by pushing things at me I had missed the first time around. But then she backed away and began pulling things on—pantyhose, bra, and dress. She walked around to the kitchen, got her galoshes and put them back in the car. Then she came back and got her new coat from the closet in the den, brought it out to the living room, and threw it on a chair. Then she sat down on the sofa, motioning me beside her. But then all of a sudden, almost in a panic, she jumped up, telling me: "If you're putting him in there, the officer when he comes, in Mrs. Howell's room, we should put sheets on the bed. Do you have any?"

I said I thought there were some in the hall closet upstairs, and we went racing up to find them. Sure enough, there they were, with a pillow case, and we came tearing down again to put them on the bed. She had just finished up and we were heading for the sofa when a car pulled up outside. When I opened the door, Mantle was getting out. "Well!" I said. "This is a pleasant surprise."

"Maybe to you," he growled.

"I'm sorry, I've been pretty nervous out here."

He came in and when he saw Jill warmed up a little. "And—speaking of pleasant surprises," he told her, shaking hands, "I guess this one helps a little."

"Deputy Mantle."

We all sat down and I offered a drink. He declined, explaining that he was on duty. I offered something to eat, but he declined that too. Then he asked some questions about the "prowler," as he called him, that the night clerk seemed to have told him about, seeming a bit puzzled by the boat we had said appeared, "and what it was doing there." I said: "If you're mixed up, it's nothing to what we were."

"It still makes no sense to me," she put in. "What on earth, what in the world—?"

"Well, in the morning we'll see," he yawned, in a way that seemed to say we'd covered it for tonight. I told him I'd show him his bedroom, and he answered that as he was on duty he couldn't go to bed, but would "lie down if I may—of course I'll take off my shoes."

I opened the door of Mom's room and suddenly he said: "Oh, I almost forgot: The clerk mentioned that you didn't have any weapon, now that we've impounded yours, so I brought you one as a temporary replacement. I agree that with all this stuff about money coming out on TV and in the papers, you need it as something to reach for in a hurry. I brought you a rifle that's been kicking around the office, an old one, like yours. Hold everything, I'll get it."

He went out and came back with a rifle. He handed it over, saying: "Clip's in the chamber, not in the barrel yet—it takes a bolt action to load."

"Oh!" she exclaimed, "it's a Springfield!" And then:

140

"Mr. Howell's is an Enfield, but I like a Springfield better." And then, at the surprised look on his face: "When I was in summer camp, they took us out on the range."

"Nice to be an expert."

He handed it over to me, and I took it through Mom's room back to the kitchen and stood it in its place inside the back door. When I got back, she was putting on her coat, he helping her. "I have to be getting back," she told me. When she'd shaken hands with him and he'd given her a pat, I took her out to her car. "Was I all right?" she whispered.

"Perfect," I told her.

"Well, if he was baffled about the boat, why wouldn't we be baffled by it?"

"That's it, something like that ought not to match up completely. When something's too good, it's not good."

"You love me?"

"I'm nuts about you."

She pulled me to her and kissed me, then let me close the door, and started the motor. She put on her lights and I stood waving as she drove off. I went back in and told Mantle where the bathroom was, showed him the thing with a handle on it under the bed, and said good night.

18

———————◆———————

I got up, dressed, and tiptoed up to the bathroom,
but the towels told me he had already been there. I
shaved, washed up, and came down, and when I went in
the living room, the door of Mom's room was open, the
bed was made up, the receptacle under the bed, if it had
ever been used, was empty, and everything was in order.
When I looked out, Mantle was standing beside his car,
talking into the phone. I opened the door and waved. He
waved back but kept talking.

When he finally came in I told him to sit down and
I'd get him some breakfast. He thanked me, but said he
would eat in town. But the way he said it was different
from the way he'd acted before, and it didn't seem that
Jill's not being there quite accounted for it. He hadn't
hid that he liked her, but after she left he'd been friendly
enough still, and it kept gnawing at me that something
had happened to him right there in the house that had
caused his change of manner. Then I thought it couldn't
be that, as nothing could have happened between his
going to bed and getting up—and decided it had to be

something caused by his phone call, perhaps some word of Mom. Later, though, I was to find out that things could happen to him, and did—right there in the house, right in Mom's room, where he had spent the night. He was writing in a notebook without looking at me. Then: "Mr. Howell, if you'll ring Miss Kreeger, and ask her to please come out for further questioning today, it'll save my having to. And I'd ring that lawyer you had—Mr. Bledsoe. Have him come out. Have her and him and yourself on hand by 11:00, when Sergeant Edgren will be ready to start—and probably Mr. Knight."

"What is this, Mr. Mantle?"

"Just matters that have come up."

"Can you give me some idea what?"

"We can and will—all in due time."

He looked at his watch, made more notes in his book, then repeated: "Eleven o'clock—I just talked to the sergeant, and he should be through by then, with some calls he'll have to put in."

"About this case?"

"Yes, of course."

"What calls?"

"All in due time. You'll know."

With kind of a wave, he went out, got in his car, and drove off. I called her at the Occidental, and we tried to figure it out, what had caused the change, from a friendly enough officer the night before to a gimlet-eyed sleuth the next day. All of a sudden she asked: "The tree—what did he say about it?"

"He didn't mention it."

"Not at all?"

"No."

143

"What did you say?"

"I was too worried about what had changed him to think about the tree. One thing at a time. When they get through with their questions, we can start up with ours."

"It's my money, though."

"It'll still be there."

"I'll feel better when I have it."

Bledsoe wasn't home. It turned out that he'd had to make a speech and had spent the night in Parkersburg. When I reached him at his office after he came in late, he didn't at all want to come out.

"I'm busy as hell and just can't spare the time." But when I told him how Mantle was acting, he decided he could after all. So around 10:00 Jill came, bringing York with her, their quarrel apparently patched up. Then Bledsoe came and we all checked it over, the little I knew to tell them, trying to figure what it was all about. York went to Mom's room and rummaged around looking for what might be there, and Jill went in and looked, but what they came up with was nothing, and what we all four figured out was the same. Then Edgren and Mantle came out in separate cars, and after them Mr. Knight in still another car. They all spoke kind of grim without really looking at us, except that Knight was grim to the officers as well as to us, as though he didn't really have faith in whatever was coming off. It wasn't much, but Bledsoe looked at me, then at Jill, and she looked at me like she wanted to throw me a wink.

But Edgren got at it at once, telling everyone to please sit down, which we did, Jill and I on the sofa, the others in chairs. He started in on me, referring to a paper he had, which I assumed was the night clerk's report, and taking me over it again, what I had said on the phone and later in person to Mantle. Something kept whispering to me: "Don't play it too smart; don't know too much." So when he asked about the boat we said we had seen, how many persons were in it, I said, "It was dark; I couldn't see." And when he asked: "How big a boat, Mr. Howell?"—I told him: "It was a rowboat, that's all I know."

"A johnboat, would you say?"

"I wouldn't say, I couldn't see."

"What did they want with the tree?"

"I don't know, you'd better ask them."

"What would you think they wanted?"

"I've told you, I don't know, but I'd give a lot to find out."

"And I'd give a lot more."

That was Jill, and Edgren snapped at her: "I wasn't asking you."

"No, but I'm telling you! Could be, it has something to do with my money, *my* money, Sergeant Edgren, not Mr. Howell's money or your money or Mr. Knight's money, but my money, and if you'd do what you're supposed to, get off your backside and start in looking, stead of sitting around here talking, we all might be better off, and specially I might be."

"I'm running this, Miss Kreeger."

"But not very well, Sergeant Edgren."

It threw him off, but not much. He sat there, measuring her up, as though trying to think what she knew. I tried to think what *he* knew and had the uneasy feeling he knew more than we knew he knew, probably connected with whatever it was that Mantle had turned up during the night. Then he turned to me once more and started in about Mom. He really worked me over, especially in regard to the day before—where I had been and why. I said: "I was looking for my stepmother over in Flint, where she used to live."

"Why? What did you want with her?"

"Remind her she was supposed to be here to answer questions."

"And what did she say to that?"

"Nothing."

"Just nothing at all?"

"That's right."

"Don't that hit you funny that you'd tell her something like that and she just told you nothing?"

"No, not at all."

"Does me."

"I don't have your sense of humor."

"Did she say whether she meant to come back?"

"No, she didn't."

"What do you mean, she didn't?"

"I mean she wasn't there."

Everyone laughed and his face got red. Bledsoe cut in then: "Sergeant, I confess myself quite surprised. This boy has gone over this again and again and again—except in regard to his stepmother. But I remind you that he's not her keeper and also that if he tried to bring her back, he was helping you, not blocking you off, and—"

"He's holding stuff back, Mr. Bledsoe."

"You think he's holding stuff back?"

"I know he's holding stuff back."

146

He motioned to Mantle who tapped a leather case and told me: "In here is a paper tape that I found in that room this morning. When I lay down I took off my necktie, shoes, and jacket. The tie I put on the chest of drawers, but this morning when I got up, it had fallen into that wastebasket in there. When I reached for it I also picked up the tape. It's a kind used in packaging money, and printed on it is 'Drover and Dealers Bank of Chicago.' And handwritten, with ballpoint, it says 'Two thousand dollars, 100 twenties, Xerox sheets Seven oo sixty-one—seven oo eighty-six.' When we called Drover and Dealers, they said those were the Xerox numbers of bills packaged up for Trans-U.S.&C., that they put in a red zipper bag and sent out for the hijacker, Shaw. They Xeroxed those bills in batches of four."

He stopped and Edgren hammered at me: "That money has been in this house. How did it get here, Howell?"

"Of that I have no idea either."

"Howell, this thing has looked queer from the start, but I'm warning you now, that further failure on your part to cooperate—"

"Hey, hey, hey," snapped Bledsoe. "Ask what you want to find out, sergeant. Stop making speeches at him."

I knew Bledsoe had to be sweating blood, as I certainly was, but at least he was acting tough. However, before any more could be said, Jill got into the act. "Mr. Howell," she told Edgren, "can't cooperate, on account he's mountain and has to stand by his kin—like this Mom character you met one day, this stepmother he's got, who stole that money, my money in case you forgot,

147

who could have brought it here and dropped that tape in the basket without his knowing about it or me knowing about it or anyone knowing but her. So how's about knocking this off, and doing what you ought to be doing, rowing up to that tree and seeing what's inside it?"

"*inside* it!"

"Some trees are hollow, you know."

"And some people know all about it without even having to look."

"A guy in a boat was looking."

"*If* he was."

"What's that supposed to mean?"

"If there *was* any boat. Maybe the time has now come for me to find you that money, so you can pretend you knew nothing about it, that it was put there by somebody else, so—"

He may have said more, and I could feel my mouth getting dry. But before he could finish, from down the river there came the sound of a horn. Mantle held up his hand, and Edgren told him: "You better see what that is. Sounds like DiVola."

Mantle slipped out, and nothing was said for a time until here he came back. "It *is* DiVola," he reported. "They want to speak to Howell."

I went out, Jill with me. The officers went out, and Bledsoe, Knight, and York went out, all stomping along the path on a beautiful spring day. When I got down to the bank, the DiVola outboard was there, with two firemen in it this time instead of three. The one in the bow was holding onto a root on the snag that was still offshore a few feet, a tree maybe a foot across, floating up in the current with roots pointing downriver, and branches dragging behind. But behind the outboard was a johnboat with oars in the locks—both boats being pulled downstream by the current, the fireman in the stern of the outboard hanging onto the johnboat's painter. "Mr. Howell, is this your boat?" asked the fireman in the bow, the one hanging to the root.

"Looks like it," I said, and when I looked around for my boat on the bank, it wasn't there. Then on the boat in the river I saw a chipped place under one oarlock that was made by a tree one day, and sang out: "Yes, that *is* my boat!"

"You're in luck, is all I have to say. It fetched up five miles down, on a float that's anchored offshore. It was headed straight for the dam. You should tie that boat up."

"I did tie it up." I shook the sapling I had made it fast to.

"Then it must have been stole," he said. "Well——there's plenty of that going on."

"So there *was* a boat!" she told Edgren, grabbing him by the shoulders and spinning him around.

"OK, OK," he answered, "but it doesn't prove anything, except—"

"Never mind what it proves," growled Knight. "There was a boat; that's the main thing."

He turned to the fireman holding onto the root, whom the other man had called Ed, and asked: "Could you gentlemen give us a little help? We want to go upstream to a tree that's up there, to a tree that may be hollow, and see what's inside of it, if anything."

Ed turned to the other man, and asked, "Rufe?"

"Sure, why not?" said Rufe.

Ed let go and Rufe gunned his motor, to shoot the boat to the bank. Then he reached the painter to me, the line from the johnboat, and I made it fast to the sapling after hauling the boat out of the bank. Then: "Who's going?" asked Ed. Knight motioned me in, and I sat on one of the two cross-seats, the one nearest the stern. He got in, taking his place beside me. Then he motioned to Edgren and Mantle who took place on the other cross-seat. Then Rufe threw the boat into reverse, and we shot downriver. He gave it full speed ahead and we started back upriver. We passed the island on the west side, kept on past my landing, and then came to the mouth of the inlet, with the tree standing in it, maybe two feet across the trunk, and white as a sycamore always is. "That's it," I said, and Rufe went in reverse. That stopped our forward motion, and when we began to slide back downriver, he cut his rudder to slew us around. Then he gave it full speed ahead, and shot us into the inlet. He throttled back, so we had slowed down when we bumped the tree. Rufe caught it and we stopped. Edgren got up then and Rufe gave him a hand to steady him while he reached into the hollow.

"There's something in there," he said, and my heart beat up, as I took it for granted, of course, that at last he'd come up with the money and that would wind it all up. But instead of lifting the bag out, he kept pulling at something inside, complaining: "The damned thing's caught."

"What is it?" asked Rufe.

"I can't tell. I don't know."

He felt around with his hand, and seemed to be spanning distance inside, then took his hand out again and spanned down outside from the rim of the hollow. He put his thumb on the spot he had measured to, then with the other hand took out his gun. "I don't know if this is going to work or not, but nothing beats a try." Then he aimed his gun at the spot and fired. Dust kicked out of the hollow and then he reached in his hand. "That did it," he said, very pleased. "Broke the splinter off." Then he came out with the strap, the one she had cut off that night, the loose end of the zipper bag strap, that had got caught in some crack inside.

"Hey!" he said, excited. "This thing's red. That corresponds with the color that zipper bag was, the one that the money was put in, for Shaw to take when he jumped. On TV they kept talking about it."

"Sure does," agreed Mantle.

"We're getting warm."

I wasn't getting warm, I was turning cold all over. "Is there anything else in there!" I asked.

"Not that I can feel," said Edgren.

He put on a glove and rummaged into the hollow. "No, that's all—but I'd call it quite a lot."

Then: "OK."

Rufe helped him once more, he stepped over Knight and me, and sat down again beside Mantle. Mantle studied the strap but didn't ask me about it, and Edgren didn't. Rufe backed us out of the inlet and into the river, headed downstream, and ran down past the island. I was trying to think what I'd say to Jill, how I could possibly tell her that Bledsoe's grand scheme that she'd put into effect to please me, had completely backfired, that her money was gone, that the boat we said we had seen had actually come during the night, that it was my boat that somebody stole and used to take what was hers. Knight stepped ashore, but I wanted to be the last and waited for Edgren and Mantle. Jill's eyes were bright as she searched us all, looking, I knew, for her money. When she didn't see it she turned to me, a question on her face. However, before I could speak, Edgren was holding the strap up. "Well young lady," he said, "you were right that the tree was hollow, and as we dope it out, your money was actually stashed there. Did you ever see this before!"

He waved the strap and she stared.

"That's been cut off that bag!" she wailed. "The bag with my money in it! . . . Where is it? What have you done with it, *say?* My bag! Where is it?"

"You'd better ask Mr. Howell."

"I'd better ask *who?*"

"Speak up, Mr. Howell."

"*I* speak up, sergeant? What are you talking about?"

"Well, it's all coming together—the paper tape in your house, the strap caught in your tree, the boat that was salvaged downstream—it seems pretty clear that though you like this girl, you like her money better. So if she wants to know where it is, like I said, she'd better ask you!"

"Dave, I can't believe it!"

"Why don't you say something, Howell?"

19

What was I going to say? The truth? That on advice
of counsel, she'd planted the money out there so he'd
find it and we'd be left in the clear? That would dig us in
even deeper without doing me any good, and besides
would backfire on Bledsoe in a way to cause him trouble.
And I knew, at the same time, that it might be just a
pitch Edgren was making, that he didn't necessarily
believe but tossed at me anyhow, to see how I reacted. I
can't pretend I came up with any answer. I was just plain
paralyzed, sweating, with my head not working at all.

Jill, though, didn't let me do any telling. She
exploded right in front of me, right in front of them all,
spilling it all, from Bledsoe's simple idea to what she had
done about it, "wading out to that tree, with the water up
to here"— motioning toward her bottom—"*icy* water up
to here—because I wanted to please him, this friendly
boyfriend of mine, because he saved my life, because he
looked like God to me at that time—was that a laugh, oh
my. And we'd hardly come ashore when this mother of
his, I'm sorry she's his stepmother, when she was

yapping about the money—that's all she thought about, and now, what do you know, *now* I find out, it's all *he* thought about! He and his lawyer friend. Yes, Mr. Bledsoe, you know who's paying you, don't you? That was an idea, wasn't it, for you to throw at me? That we'd put my money back, in that tree where we had found it, so the sheriff's men would find it, and then no one could say we'd known where it was all along. And fool that I was, I did what you said exactly, with water—"

"Up to *there!*" snapped Bledsoe. "Was your backside bare, may I ask?"

"You better believe it was."

"I wish I'd been there!"

That got a laugh but didn't stop Edgren from staring over what he'd turned up, without having known that he would. He interrupted to ask: "Do you mean you planted that money? Out there, for us? On Mr. Bledsoe's advice?"

"Do I have to go over it twice? OK, if I have to, I will. Yes, that's what I mean. Little did I realize the reason that he had for giving me that advice."

"And when was it that you—?"

But Knight cut him off. "She was his client," he snapped, "and it was her money. If what he advised her to do was on the side of the law, to make possible the finding of what you'd been looking for, there was nothing wrong with it, nothing unethical—any lawyer might have done it."

"But when Howell took the money—"

"What proof do you have of that? If you're charging him with that theft, I'm the one who must face a judge, at a habeas corpus hearing, a judge who doesn't like it, being hauled out of bed at night, and defend the charge of yours. So far, you have no proof that Howell did anything except kill a man who damned well deserved to die. Your job is to find that woman—Mrs. Howell, I believe was her name—who could be the one, it appears, who hid that money in the first place, and until you do—"

"OK, OK."

"It could be what you think."

"Sir, I said OK."

"It doesn't have to be."

That shut Edgren up but not Jill. She raved on and on, damning me, damning Bledsoe, saying over and over what she'd said before. In the middle of her show I was startled to see my mother, standing out on the edges, halfway back of Mantle, as though she'd been there some time. She looked perfectly beautiful, pale in the sunlight, a red ribbon on her hair, a short dress showing her legs, the mink coat carelessly thrown over her shoulder. Edgren saw her about the time I did and wasn't nice about it. "Madam," he said, "this is a sheriff's investigation. If you don't mind, we'd prefer not having a gallery."

But at that I broke, perhaps from the strain I'd been under, and blew my top. "Sergeant," I bellowed, "this is my place, and I'll say who stays and who doesn't. This lady's my mother. She stays."

"Not if I say she doesn't."

"Goddamn it, I say she does!"

"Howell, I warn you that use of such language to an officer of the law is a misdemeanor in this state, and—"

"For Jesus Christ's sake, how often do I have to say it?"

"You know who has that money?" she asked Edgren, as he was drawing breath to speak.

"What's it to you what I know?"

"I do know, that's what."

The change in Edgren's expression, in Jill's expression, in everyone's expression, was funny to see, or would have been if anything could have been then. She looked calmly from one to the other and finally wound up studying Jill. "Well, Jill?" she asked, "what do you say to that?"

"I don't really know."

"Makes a difference, doesn't it? A moment back, you were telling the world, at the top of your lungs, and your lungs have quite a top. Now you don't know what to say. I know, I think I know, who took your money last night. It wasn't Dave. You knew that, didn't you? Knew it all along?"

"I didn't *want* to believe it."

"Answer me. You knew it wasn't Dave, didn't you?"

"OK, then, I did."

"But you had to blame someone—?"

"Maybe."

"But now that you think I know where your money is, who took it last night, you're willing to calm down—?"

"What are you getting at?"

"I just wanted to know."

And then, to Edgren: "Sergeant, I know, I have to admit, Mrs. Howell took that money, my cousin, my son Dave's stepmother. I don't think she has it now. I told Dave yesterday, there's something very peculiar about her disappearance that complicates things for you, yet perhaps, in a way simplifies them for me. Sergeant, I think my cousin is dead. She hasn't turned up in Flint, the coal camp that was her home, and I simply can't imagine her driving off without taking that money. Someone took it last night, that much I know, but I don't think she was the one. OK, I'm going to assume she *is* dead. That'll cut me loose from all duty to stand by my kin and leave me free to help you—if you want my help."

It was Knight who walked over and took her hand with quite a courtly bow. Everyone was standing around wondering what to do next. The firemen were in their boat watching Edgren, maybe for some kind of sign, what he wanted of them next.

And then, all of a sudden Rufe opened his mouth and let go right in the river, a gush of yellow vomit splashing down. Everyone stared at him, and then a sickening smell floated in. Then Jill screamed and we saw this horrible thing, with a belly big as a barrel, arms sticking up, and eyes popping out of its head. I knew it was Mom, just from the glimpse I got, before turning away and swallowing hard to keep my stomach down.

I could hear Rufe telling Knight: "I know what the answer is: she's the one that took out the boat, that last time we were here, and capsized it on that tree—when Mr. Howell thought, and we supposed that the boat had floated off on a rise of the river, and hung up on the tree, just by its own self."

Just then Rufe gave a yell: "It's broke loose, it's going downstream—that corpse I'm talking about!"

Sure enough, out of the corner of my eye I could see it, spinning around in the current, down past the roots of the tree. Now it was no longer tangled up in the branches. Rufe started his engine again and Ed picked up a boat hook. Rufe steered around the snag, cut sharp to pass the island, and then shot downriver fast. Ed jabbed two or three times with the hook, and finally caught it in something. I couldn't see what. He had to work the hook around the bow while Rufe let the motor idle. Then Rufe brought the boat into the bank, and Mantle yanked out the corpse, letting go real quick and stumbling off to the bushes. "You know who it is, Howell?" Edgren asked, turning to me.

"My stepmother," I said.

"Then, if you'll look at her, you can identify her, and we'll take it from there."

"I can't look at her!"

"I'm sorry, but you'll have to."

"I can't, I won't."

"I'll identify," said my mother.

"I'm sorry madam, it has to be done by a relative."

"I am a relative, closer than he is. She was my second cousin. He was her nephew twice removed, though she raised him as his stepmother. I said I'd identify."

The way she said it meant business and Knight motioned to Edgren. My back was to her and the corpse but I heard her recite: "This was Mrs. Myra Giles Howell, widow of Jody Howell, age about 38, no close kin except for her stepson, my son, David Howell, and a brother, Sidney Giles, address Flint, West Virginia. Her address this property here, highway 60, Marietta, Ohio."

"That covers it, thank you, ma'am."

Edgren was most respectful. "Now," she went on,

stepping off to one side, her handkerchief to her nose, "I think we should go to the ranchhouse, that place you see up there, the original one she lived in, and see if her car is there—my son's car, actually. Apparently, as this gentleman"—nodding toward Rufe— "has kindly figured it, she drowned when the boat capsized after she took it out, we would assume to pick up the money, where she'd hid it in that tree. But she left home in the car, and if we find it, that will explain, I think, most of what happened that night."

By that time, after a whispered conversation with Edgren, Mantle had left, I supposed to phone in from his car, for the undertaker to be called, and maybe the coroner notified. He was now trotting up the path, and Edgren, after a glance in his direction, told my mother: "OK, soon as Officer Mantle gets back. Someone must stay with this body, and—"

"Can do, can do," Rufe chirped up, very friendly. "We'll stand by, if you want. You don't mind if we move upwind a little way? Like to the island, maybe."

"Of course not," said Edgren. "Thanks." Then: "OK," he told my mother.

So we all headed for the ranchhouse, he and my mother leading, Bledsoe and Knight following along behind, and York following them, with me. And sure enough, soon as we passed the kitchen there was my car, parked between it and the house. When I opened the door, Mom's bag was on the seat, and her keys were in the ignition. Edgren had me open the house, and then open the kitchen, so he could search, as he did once before. I think he hoped he might find the money. When he came out my mother told him: "Now, if you want my help, I have to tell you I could do without yours for a while. There are people I have to see, to find out what they know, and they're the kind of people who won't come in to talk if police cars are parked outside."

"You want us to leave?"

"If it's not asking too much."

Knight nodded. "OK," said Edgren. "We'll clear out soon as we've cleared the undertaker, when he comes for that corpse. By now, Officer Mantle has put in the call."

"And one other thing: I'll have to be using that phone for some fairly personal calls. I have to know if it's bugged."

"Well, madam, as to that, we don't give out information—"

"*Is it bugged?*" Her voice snapped.

"No, ma'am, it's not."

"That's what I want to know."

Knight eyed her, Bledsoe eyed her, York eyed her, Jill eyed her, and Edgren did. It was no trouble to see who was running the show. She thought a minute, then said: "Now, Dave, if you'll drive us over—I think Jill can ride with us—we can get busy with what we have to do. First, we could use some lunch—or at least *I* could."

I got in and she opened the other door, standing aside for Jill. "You ride in the middle," she whispered.

"*You* ride in the middle," I snapped. "let her ride by the door."

Mother hesitated, then got in. Jill said: "I don't have to ride at all!"

"OK, then, walk," I told her.

I reached over Mother and closed the door, then

pulled out after starting the motor. "You weren't very nice to her," said my mother.

"I wasn't trying to be."

"She's a very sweet girl."

"She's a rotten little bitch."

"She had some provocation."

"What provocation?"

"When you lose a hundred thousand dollars—"

"Ninety-eight thousand dollars."

"When you lose $98,000, you'll find out, all by yourself, what it can do to you—your temper, your love, your everything."

"She called me a thief."

"Did the officers call you that first?"

"Does she have to call me everything they think up?"

"It makes a difference."

"Not to me."

20

All the cars were still there, but we parked and went inside. I went back to the kitchen to get her something to eat, but she put her arms around me and edged me back to the living room. "I'll take over," she said. "You've been put through the wringer—sit down and I'll bring you something." A fire was built and I lit it. Pretty soon she came in with some lunch—a couple of ham sandwiches, some pie, milk, and coffee. We sat there eating, and one by one the cars left, the officers ringing the bell, to tell me "stand by," as usual, and to wish her luck with her looking, in a most respectful way.

Bledsoe did the same, being much upset still, and then Santos was there, after supervising his men, as they shoved something wrapped in a tarp into his dead wagon. He checked it over with me, the cemetery lot we had, that Mr. Howell was buried in, the kind of casket I wanted, and so on. He gave it to me quick, the arrangements they'd made for the inquest, "which will now be kind of a double." While he was talking, Knight rang the bell to explain it to me from his angle. After he left Jill showed, from the path that led from the ranchhouse, York behind her, but they got in their cars and drove off without ringing the bell.

When Santos left, that seemed to be all, but when Mother finished eating she jumped up and picked up the phone, saying: "I have to call Sid and get him over here."

"What for?" I asked, sounding sour in spite of myself.

"The money," she answered.

"To hell with the money," I snapped, "and once more, to hell with her. Who's paying you to get it back? She's not, I promise you."

"It's not her. If who took it is who I think, they're a Giles from Flint, and turned on her the selfsame way they turned on other Gileses three years and more ago. I have to get them for that."

"And Sid knows who they are?"

"Sid knows everything."

"I could do without him."

"I couldn't, not today. I need him."

She had dialed and now someone answered, a child from what I could hear. Sid wasn't married, but he had what he called a housekeeper, kind of a fleshy-looking woman who had a couple of children. My mother asked for Sid, and the answer seemed to be he'd gone to Marietta. She left word if he should call, then hung up and came back, to sit with me on the sofa. She picked up my hand and kissed it, and all of a sudden the day melted off, and it was just her and me, in a moment of beautiful peace. I said: "Well, here we are."

"Yes, darling. And I love it."

"Me too—but who are we?"

"What do you mean, who are we?"

"We know who you are, of course, but who am I? Mother, who is my father?"

She closed her eyes, as though in pain, and when she opened them didn't look at me, but stared straight ahead. Then: "Dave, your father's a very big man, one you're going to be proud of, when he finally makes himself known. But my lips have been sealed all these years, on account of his wife—this girl he had married shortly before he met me, who got sick almost at once, and after that wasn't a wife, but an invalid dependent he couldn't turn his back on—at least as he thought. She was dying. She still is—22 years have gone by, and she's still dying, Dave. She had a stroke that made her as helpless as a baby and she stays out there in Arizona, where she lives with her nurse."

She closed her eyes again, beat her knee with her fist, and moaned: "I shouldn't talk that way. I sound as though I want her to hurry up, and I mustn't! And yet I can't help it, I do! I want him! I want him all to myself! I want an end of this secret we have!"

"Why doesn't he get a divorce?"

"He won't cast her off."

"It doesn't matter to her—not so good for you. Why should he put her ahead of you?"

"I asked him that once; I screamed it at him. I can be pretty rotten. I come from Flint, West Virginia. He shut me up, though. So I had to calm down, and did. Know what he said, Dave?"

"What?"

"'She has to die.'"

"That shuts me up, too." And then: "You're going to be married, though, soon as she does die?"

"I think so."

"Don't you know?"

"Dave, we discuss it often. You have to understand. We live together. We have a beautiful home on the river in Indianapolis. He introduces me to his friends. We entertain them together. Of course, for how it looks, I have a house of my own, next door, so I'm just a friend. I have no reason to fear, to suspect him at all, and yet—I'm a woman, Dave. I'll believe it when I see it, when I'm looking at that ring he puts on my finger."

Sid called about that time. When I answered, he talked quite friendly, as though he'd forgotten about our run-in or at least didn't hold it against me. Then I called her to the phone and she talked friendly too: "Sid, I have to see you! Something's happened. It's about Little Myra, but I can't tell you what on account of this phone. It's bugged, as we know, so I have to mind how I talk. But I have to see you, Sid. I'd rather you come out here." She broke off then and listened, and he talked for some little time, apparently trying to find out what she was talking about. She kept coming back to how the phone was bugged, and after a while, told him very nice: "Thanks, Sid. I knew I could count on you. I wouldn't ask it if I didn't feel I had to."

Pretty soon she hung up, but didn't come back, with me on the sofa. She started walking around the room, and I sat there admiring her shape and the way she walked, kind of limber-kneed, so she halfway floated, and you noticed it, how willowy she was. Suddenly I said: "You didn't tell him she was dead."

"What he doesn't know won't hurt him."

It didn't seem to be something she'd have to hold back on account of the bug on the phone—and especially not if there was no bug on the phone. Little by little I figured it out, that so long as he didn't know, he'd have to come to find out how things stood. I began to wonder if Sid was the guy she was after.

21

All of a sudden she asked me for paper, and I got her a tablet I had. She got a ballpoint out of her bag and began writing. Then she got up and stared out the front window. I looked, and a car was just turning in from the highway to the lane. She tore off the sheet she'd been writing on, put it in her bag, and handed the tablet to me. I put it back in the table drawer. The car was Uncle Sid's, and it came in to the loop in front of the house, then rolled halfway around it. Then it cut inside the loop, circled around my Dodge and my mother's car, and wound up parking in front of them. It was a funny thing to do, and I saw no reason for it, but the look on her face as she watched from the window showed that she did. Uncle Sid got out, and she opened the door herself to let him in. She took him in her arms, held him close, and exclaimed, "Sid, Sid, Sid! At last, at last, you've come! I'm so glad to see you, so glad!"

He held her close too, said: "Myra, hi," "Gee you're looking good," and other dumb stuff. Then: "Myra, last I heard of my sister was a couple of nights ago, when I drove on up from Flint, after reading that stuff in the paper, and David said she had left—got in a row with that girl, or over that girl, whatever it was, and drove off. I supposed she was headed for home. Flint was where she'd naturally head for, and waited and waited and waited. But she hasn't come." And then, after studying my mother's face: "Myra? What's happened?"

"Little Myra's dead. She drowned."

"She—did you say drowned?"

The way he said it, I had the feeling he'd learned it by heart, that it was an act, that he'd known all along, she was drowned, or if he didn't know it, he'd guessed it. He sounded phoney. But my mother went over and touched him, as though he was really shook, and recited it all straight: "Drowned, Sid, that's right. They recovered her body today, where she was caught on a tree limb, in under the surface, somehow."

He listened, occasionally shaking his head, dropping his face in his hands, and getting his handkerchief out to wipe his eyes, which weren't wet that I could see, but he wiped them anyway. "So," she wound up, "it's been a blow, as you can easily understand, she being the only one besides Jody Howell, who knew the truth about David—we weren't too close before, but after she took him it brought us as close as two women ever get. *But* there's more. We got work to do, you and I."

"Not so fast," he whispered. "Give me a minute, Myra. I'm not used to it yet." And then to me: "Can I borrow the phone?"

I told him to help himself and he went and picked it up, first putting a dollar down. He dialed, then talked, I couldn't tell who to. He mumbled what had happened,

"Better tell them, better tell them all. It's going to come out anyhow. No use keeping it quiet. I'll be home, but late. Real late—may be some time before I can leave."

He came back to his seat, and then at last, in a natural tone of voice, asked my mother: "Yes, Myra? What kind of work? What are you talking about?"

"That poke, Sid. That poke of money she took, Little Myra, I mean. The one the hijacker had."

"She took that poke?"

"That's right, Sid."

"Well, wait a minute. There was stuff in the papers about it, how the officers weren't satisfied, the whole story was told, but—how did she get in it? Who says she took the poke?"

"I do, Sid."

"And what do you have to go on?"

"There were exactly three of them there—Dave, the girl, and her. It wasn't David. It wasn't the girl. So it had to be her."

"How do you know who it wasn't?"

"I have David's word for it."

"Which you'll take, I think," I said, causing a terrific explosion. My mother turned on me and screamed: "Will you kindly keep your mouth shut? Will you let me talk without messing in? Will you for once in your life shut up?"

"Sure I will."

I snapped it pretty mean and she came over and slapped my face. "And who says anyone took it?" asked Sid, as though nothing at all had been said. "The way the papers told it, that poke got dunked in the river."

"It did not."

"Once more, how do you know?"

"It's all been checked out—the officer, the one who stayed here last night, found the wrapper in the morning, the paper tape from the bank, from one of the packs of bills. She must have brought it here. If so, that poke didn't get dunked."

"So, OK, but where do we come in? If she had the poke with her, if she had it when she left, then it did get dunked after all—when she did."

"It did not get dunked, Sid."

She told the rest, about Jill finding the money while trying to catch a fish, her putting it back, and what happened later—the fireman finding the boat and the rest. "Whoever that thief was, he rowed up in that boat after stealing it and grabbed that poke. And that's where we come in. We have to get it back—the poke and the money that's in it."

"Why do we?"

"The day after it happened, after the hijacker got it, after David let him have it, the president of the company, Morgan I think his name is, deeded the girl that money, so it couldn't make trouble for her. So it's hers now. So she's going to be one of us, soon as she marries David."

I opened my mouth once more to say it was off, that I had no interest in Jill—but after what had happened once when I put my mouth in, I decided to postpone my remark. Uncle Sid looked at me, said: "Yeah, I kind of thought it was something like that." And then, to my mother: "I'd say OK, of course—there couldn't be any question, if there was something I could do. But I swear, I don't think of anything."

"I do. There is something, Sid."

She opened her bag and took out the sheet of paper, the one she'd torn from my tablet, with the stuff she'd written on it. "I suspect this man," she said, "and here's what I want you to do: Get on his tail at once. Camp out on him where he lives, on the river road there near Huntington. Park up the street from his house and keep watch on this dirty rat—where he goes, what he does, most of all, how he spends the money. With $98,000 to play around with, he's bound to do some playing—on the horses, girls, booze. When you have something to tell me, let me know and I'll take it from there."

He sat blinking, first at the paper, then at her, and then said: "Myra, you're asking something of me I don't in any way like—it's not in my line. I don't know the first thing about it, and it's on behalf of someone, that girl I'm talking about, who means nothing to me."

"She's going to be one of us, Sid."

"OK, then, OK. *When* she is, when I get to know her, when I get to like her, *if* I get to like her—then we'll talk. Until then I have to say no."

"Then could be too late—no use nailing him *after* he's stashed the money."

"Myra, I still say no."

She pulled her chair nearer to his, then talked a little lower, as though just for him, with me left out. "Sid," she said, real friendly, "I haven't said all, not quite. I wouldn't have that much nerve, to ask something like this and expect you to pay for it, your meals, your room in one of those motels, your gas and oil and tips—so, of course, I equalize, I should have mentioned it sooner." She opened her bag and began taking tens off a roll, laying them beside him, there on the sofa—quite a pile, maybe 10 or 12. She said: "I have some I can share, cash that was slipped me, and I'll be only too glad. . . ."

I could feel she was up to something, and let her play it along, but at the same time, I was beginning to feel pretty nervous. Sid stared at the bills, and what went through his mind I don't know, maybe that if he picked them up, no one would ever know what he actually used them for. Anyway, he did, straightening them up in a little pack, neat. Then he took out his wallet to slip them in.

I've said she had moved in close, so she was now knee-to-knee. Suddenly she slapped that billfold, so it bounced on the table and landed on the floor, in front of the TV set. He jumped up and started after it, but I stepped in between. He wrestled me, but I dumped him back on the sofa. My mother, first smoothing her dress, picked up the wallet, then knelt by the table, and started counting what was in it. It seemed mainly to be $20 bills, and when she'd counted them all, she said: "OK, Sid, that says it, I flushed it out—100 twenties, exactly what she took with her, when she banged out of this house, and what must have been still in her bag when you went through it last night there at the other house, before walking down, stealing that boat, and taking the bag from that tree. OK, Sid, where is it?"

She looked up at last, and I looked up—into a blue .45 automatic Sid was leveling at her, holding it on his knee.

22

Motioning with the gun, he marched us back to our seats, to our chairs, on the other side of the table, beside the TV set. Then with one hand he picked up the twenties. Folding them, he slipped them in his coat pocket. He picked up the wallet and slipped that in. Still with his eyes on my mother, he bent both knees and pawed around on the floor, for the tens, which had slipped down there. He got them, stood up, and walked over to my mother, dropping them in her lap. Then: "OK, you lying, thieving bitch," he began, but I cut in: "Watch your language, Sid."

He did a quarter turn with the gun, to point it at me. "I called her a lying, thieving bitch," he said. "What do you call her?"

"I call her my mother," I growled. "And you better."

"I call her a lying, thieving bitch, and on top of that a filthy whore. And you don't say any different, do you? *Do you?*"

His voice was pure bile, and I made no answer. I measured with my eye how far I was from him, and whether I could make it before he could shoot. But my eyes must have tipped him. He did another quarter turn, quick, so the gun was on me, to mean it. "Don't move!" he snapped. "Stay right where you're at, kid."

He went back to the sofa, sat down, then suddenly ordered us: "Lock hands! Put them in front! On your knees, where I can see them! *And lock them!*"

We did as he said.

"OK, where is it?" he asked.

"Where is what?" asked my mother.

"The poke! What do you think?"

"You have it, Sid. You tell *me*, why don't you?"

"You got the goddamn gall to sit there and tell me that? After you lined it out for me, word for word, after you all but owned up it was you who took that poke?"

"*I all but owned up?* Sid, I always thought you were crazy, but not that crazy, oh no! What do you mean, I all but owned up?"

"Last night, so you said, you were here and then you left. For God's sake, Myra, who knew about that boat? Where it was and how to get to it? Who knew about the tree? Where *it* was and how to get to *it?* Who do you think you're fooling?"

"OK, Sid, but the thing of it is, I'm not like you, thank God. I wouldn't go back on my kin, on a girl who will be my kin. I couldn't do that to her."

"What do you mean, you're not like me?"

"You know what I mean, Sid. If you don't, drop the nose of that gun and I'll tell you."

He angled the gun at the floor, and she said: "I'm talking about those boys, those two cousins of yours, that you turned on year before last and left to die in that mine

174

you're caretaker of. They were your partners, weren't they? In that business of yours? You brought them over, didn't you? From Logan? To help out in that mine, share and share alike?"

Now his business, as I've said, was booze—moonshine, it used to be called, except the way they do it now, mixing corn and rye, and letting it color in charred kegs, it's more like regular bourbon, and the bars in Ohio grab it on account of the low price. "And suppose I did, what then?" he snapped. "What's that got to do with the bag?"

It was some time before she answered him. She sat staring at him, like trying to screw up her nerve to say whatever it was that was still on her mind. Outside a car drove up, then passed the three cars on the loop, my car, my mother's car, and Sid's car, then drove off again without stopping. I didn't pay much attention, remembering what she had said about people that wouldn't come in if they saw certain cars out front. Turned out that was the reason, but in a way different from what she had meant, and a lot more important.

"It's got to do with a rat, leaving his kin to die, so he could keep their share of the bundle of money they'd made."

She said it at last, and it was Sid's turn to stare, as though figuring how much she knew. Then, kind of hoarse, he asked: "When did I do that?"

"The day the top fell down in that dead entry you used to get to the still you had, in the old Ajax number three—as everything started to shake, when the strip shovel started up on the other side of the mountain. With that top blocking passage, it meant those boys were trapped. But they could have been saved, couldn't they?

Could have been gotten out, if you'd put in a call about them, to Ajax, the police, or someone. But no! That would have tied you in to the still, and besides, there was the cash, the money that had piled up, that still hadn't been split. So you didn't call, did you? You just walked away from those boys, said they'd gone West in their car, let them stay in that mine—which is where they are now, isn't it? *Isn't it!*"

There was a long argument then, but what they said I don't rightly recall, as I suddenly had the feeling, whether from something I heard, or from a hunch I had, that something was behind me, out there in the hall. And I must have made some motion or tipped it where my mind was, because instead of answering her, he whipped the gun around, so it pointed straight at my gut, and told me: "Stay where you're at! Don't move or you get it!"

I stayed where I was, I promise you, but I kept trying to think what was next on his schedule, as bringing someone in, someone to sneak up behind us, didn't seem to make sense, unless he wanted help carrying bodies down to the river or something like that. However, all I actually did, with that gun looking at me, was sit there, without moving, as he said. In a moment he turned back to my mother, telling her: "I don't have to answer you." And then: "Do I?"

"I guess not," she whispered.

"Is that all?"

"Yes, that's all."

"I thought it was."

He patted the gun, said "Now" as though getting ready to talk, and let a grin spread over his face. But at that she really exploded: "It's not all, it's not all! I haven't even started yet!"

"Oh yes you have—it's all!"

"Mother," I couldn't help saying, "for God's sake!"

"It's not all. I'm going to say it and nothing can stop me! You said they'd left for the West, that they'd driven off in their car—but there their car was at your house. So you hid it in the woods and that night drove it here. And next day, when David had gone in to work, you let her show you where, and toppled it into the river. But that left the money, which if found on you could have got you 20 years in prison. And she put it away for you, with you rowing the johnboat, in that place where she hid that bag, in that very selfsame tree you knew she'd use, to hide something in a hurry. So you knew where the poke was, so you took it. *Didn't you?*"

"Myra, for the second and I hope the last time, I don't have to answer on every crazy thing you dream up."

"I didn't dream about your money in that tree. Myra told me."

"Goddamn it, shut up!"

"Sid, where's the poke?"

"That's what we're going to find out."

"How? Find out?"

"We're searching your car, that's how."

He got up, motioning at us, with the gun, to head for the front door. I edged toward it, but she didn't. She got up, turned her back on him, and picked the mink coat up, where it was spread on a chair at the far end of the room. She was slipping it on with a little go-to-hell smile, when suddenly he burst out: "Being a rat to my kin, hey?—and look, just look who's talking! Myra, you got a gall, you got a nerve, to say what you did, the trick you played on her—on Little Myra, my sister, your cousin, your kin. Having this goddamn bastard, right there in Marietta, and then putting it on her! Saying she was the one, and making her raise him for you! Oh yes you did, and she had to—she couldn't turn down the money, that clinker she was going to marry, little as he made or ever would make in his life. So, looking you in the eye and meaning every word, I say you're a whore."

"I say you're a thief."

"Come on!"

It was around 6:30, still daylight, when we went out front, and I looked around for the other car that had driven up in the hope I could yell for help and have them go call the officers. But it wasn't anywhere in sight. Sid chunked my ribs with the gun and told me to open my car. I did and he looked inside, finding nothing, of course. Then he told Mother to open her car. She did and he looked again. Two dresses were hanging up, in front of the back seat. He used the gun to flip them, but of course saw nothing behind them. Then he said: "OK, kid, I'm going to open my car, and *you're* going to search it, see?"

He handed me his keys, and when I hesitated, chunked the gun into my ribs once more. I did as he said, opening the doors. It was a buzzard's roost inside, full of all kinds of stuff, a case of empty bottles, magazines, a hacksaw, coils of rubber tubing, a bra, anything you could think of—but no bag. He had me open the trunk, and no bag was there, either. He snapped the trunk lid down, locked it, and snarled: "Get in the house, you two! Get in and close the door! Get in there and stay there, or I'm letting you have it!"

"Letting *us* have it!" she half whispered, "that's what *he* thinks! I'm letting *him* have it, now—if it's the last thing I do on this earth!" She went out in the hall and back to the kitchen, then at once came whirling back. "What did you do with it?" she half screamed at me. "In God's name, Dave, where is it?"

"*What?*"

"That rifle!"

"What the hell? I didn't do anything with it!"

"It's not there!"

She went to the front door to look out. A shot came from outside, splintering the lintel over her head. She dropped to the floor while I went to the window to look. By then he was circling the loop, and it suddenly was made clear why he'd parked as he had, ahead of the other cars. He wanted to have a clear track if he had to get out quick. He rolled on, then came to the lane and turned into it. That's when she grabbed my arm.

Because there from the side of the house, in the gathering dark, came a shadow I didn't recognize. Then I could see it was Jill, carrying the Springfield. She took a few steps, then stopped. Then she planted herself and raised the rifle. For a long second she didn't move. Then fire cut the twilight, and there came that sharp little crack a rifle makes when fired outdoors. Then the left rear tire of Sid's car coughed, wobbled, and went flat. He kept on going, turning from the loop into the lane. He opened up to gain speed, but the car started to buck.

Then it yawed, as the front wheels cut left. Then it started to slide, down the gully beside the lane. Then suddenly it toppled, with all four wheels in the air, the front two spinning around. The top of the car had been mashed as flat as the hood and trunk. By that time, my mother and I had run out, and Jill was there in the lane, screaming and weeping, and pointing, at what was under the car—or on top of it, actually, as it stuck there, upside down. "There it is!" she yelped at the top of her lungs. "Oh please! Help me! Before it catches fire and burns up!"

And sure enough, there was the zipper bag, tied by its strap to the intake pipe of the tank and safe from all ordinary search. She began clawing at it, but it was knotted hard, and she kept breaking her fingernails and shaking them and sucking them. I took out my knife and started to open it, to cut the strap loose for her. But I changed my mind as I happened just then to remember what she'd accused me of. I stood there and watched her claw. At last she got the strap loose, grabbed the bag to her chest, and cuddled it as though it was a newborn child or something. She broke down in my mother's arms, letting go of the rifle. I caught it as it fell, and my mother said: "Dave, stand by while I take her inside and get her calmed down. I'll call the sheriff's office. They'll have to take charge of this. But Sid's still in that car and he still has that gun. Watch him—watch him every minute."

She took Jill in the house but not till she'd held her close and whispered in her ear: "I'm proud of you, Jill. You did it just right, our way, the mountain way, the way

I wanted to." And then, to me: "She's one of us now, Dave."

"Who is *us?*" I heard myself growl. "If you're talking about me, leave me out."

"You bet I'm leaving you out!" snapped Jill. "Why didn't you lend me that knife? I saw you take it out. You had it right in your hand! Why didn't you pass it to me?"

"Why should I lend you a knife? It's your money, it's what you care about—far be it for me to sully it up with my hands or my well-sullied knife."

"Dave!" screamed my mother.

"Take her inside!" I bellowed, "or you got a job on your hands, getting me calmed down!"

23

As they went in the house Jill was wailing: "He has two thousand dollars of mine right in his wallet. If that car burns up, I'll lose it!" And I thought to myself: If I ever was sick of something, it's that two thousand dollars and all the rest of the dough. My mother took her inside and for a half hour or more, after my mother called out the door, "They're on their way!" there was nothing for me to do but patrol up and down with the rifle, now and then calling to Sid, to find out how he was, and if there was some way that I could get him out. However, no answer came from the crumpled interior of the car. Then at last, turning into the lane was a car with Edgren and Mantle in it, leading a tow car in, and following that an ambulance. First thing was to right the overturned car, which was tough, as the tow car had to cut over, into the open field, run their tow line across, shackle on to an axle, and pull. But the ground was soft from being wet in spring, and its wheels kept spinning around, digging in deeper and deeper, so for a moment it looked like it was going to need help to get out, too. But all of a sudden Sid's car banged down on its wheels and the intern, the one who came with the ambulance, opened the door. At once he stepped back, making a sign like an umpire calling a runner safe, and said: "That's it!" Then: "OK, we'll take him in. Where to? Which undertaker?"

"Santos," Edgren told him.

When the ambulance had gone off and the tow car had gone off hauling what was left of Sid's car behind it, Edgren and Mantle came in the house to question me, my mother, and Jill, but mainly Jill. Edgren, now that the case was solved, and in a way that did not make him look silly at all, was nice as pie to Jill, coming back to it several times: "You had reason to think that this man had taken your money, that he had it in the car, and you shot his tire out to stop him. What reason did you have to think so?"

She said she had driven out to the house, "to talk some more to this lady, find how things were going, whether she'd heard anything, or had something to tell me. Then I saw this car, and remembered it from before, when that man Giles had come and Mr. Howell had kicked him out. So I kept right on around, around the loop I mean, passing the other cars, and started back toward the highway. But then I thought I'd better go back and see what's going on. So I parked at the side of the lane and slid down in the gully. I followed it around, then cut to the back of the house and went in the kitchen door. I took care to make no noise, and went through the hall, till I was close to the arch, that one there, where I could hear what was being said. Then here all three of them came, on their way out to the cars, and I stepped in under the stairs. I was pretty scared, as I thought that man might kill me—my second close call of that kind, all in less than a week. But he didn't, and soon as all three were out I ducked back to the kitchen, grabbed that rifle and went outside. I kept close to the house, and heard him order them back, Mr. Howell and his mother, into the house again. Soon as he started his car I pulled the bolt and got ready. And then—"

"Just a minute," Edgren cut in. "You knew this man was armed, and shot out his tire as one way of protecting yourself, of saving your life perhaps—"

"Something like that," she answered. "I'd a lot rather that man should stop and look down the barrel of my gun, instead of me looking down his."

"OK," said Edgren. He turned to Mantle, who looked at the notes he'd been taking. "That covers it," he said, "except for one thing: From what Mr. Howell has told us and what his mother has said, when this man's wallet is searched, a flock of twenties will be in it, maybe a hundred, amounting to two thousand bucks. Do you claim that money as yours?"

"I hope to tell you I do."

Jill banged it back real quick, and Mantle played his ballpoint on his teeth. "You have any proof it belongs to you?" he asked her.

She started to tell how Mr. Morgan had given it to her, but then stopped, seeing right away that that wasn't the trouble. What had to be proved was that the two thousand bucks in the wallet was part of the Morgan gift. They all three looked at each other and I guess I got in it. "You impounded the proof of this money," I told Edgren. "On that tape Officer Mantle found was the

184

record of copies made, of the Xerox pictures they took, of the bills that tape was around, and—"

"They'll show it," he cut in. "That's right, that makes it simple. We call Chicago, they look up their Xerox pictures, get us the numbers—and that does it. OK, that straightens us out." Then: "Are we done?" he asked Mantle.

"Not quite," Mantle answered, clicking his pen on his teeth once more. "Her shooting his tire out was justifiable, along the line of a citizen's arrest, if she knew he had her money. But as it hadn't been found, she didn't know it, really. But, on the basis of what she heard, listening in from the hall, she knew, she knew for certain, that whether he had the big pot, the cash in the zipper bag, he did have that two thousand bucks, in twenties there in his wallet—and she had to know it was hers—"

"So there was a corpus delicti," said Edgren, "a corpus she knew about." And then, to Jill: "A corpus delicti, miss, doesn't always mean a body. It generally means that, too, but mainly it means evidence a crime was committed."

"And it's important," said Mantle, pretty solemn. "In this case, especially."

"Very important," said Edgren.

"Thanks, Dave!" sobbed Jill, coming over and grabbing my hand. However, I shook her off. "I don't want your thanks," I told her, "or any part of you." She crumpled up on the sofa and really started to bawl. "Dave," snapped my mother, "you must be under a strain—I think you forget yourself. If you're going to marry this girl—?"

"I'm not! Stop trying to say I am!"

By then Edgren and Mantle were at the door. Edgren made a stiff little speech: "Thanks ever so much, Mrs. Howell," he began.

"Miss Giles," she corrected.

"Mrs. Giles, I'm sorry."

"Miss Giles, I'm not married."

"Miss Giles, for being so cooperative."

My mother bowed, her face set, as though it was chiseled in marble.

"Mr. Howell, thanks for your help, and Miss Kreeger—"

But all Jill did was bawl, and on that pleasing note the officers finally left.

24

So, not to string it out, they had the inquest Tuesday, by now a week late, kind of a triple, in one of Santos' parlors, with the coroner, Dr. Snyder, a jury of six people pulled in from the street, Mr. Knight, for the state's attorney's office, and Mr. Bledsoe, for my mother, Jill, and me. And three verdicts were brought, two of homicide, justifiable, and one of accident, by drowning, with nobody held. So that rang down the curtain, and the three of us walked out free.

Then one thing happened that I'll get to, but after that nothing at all for two or three months. My mother went back to Indianapolis and called often but didn't come out any more. Then, however, things happened and happened fast. The wire came from Arizona, and my father at last was free. So in a few days he and my mother got married, and showed up in his car, a big Rolls limousine, with him and my mother in back, and his secretary and the driver up front—with grins on everyone's face and an invitation to the bridal supper in one of Marietta's swank hotels. His name, it turned out, is John Gilmore Rider, who I'd heard of as the president of Husky Bus Lines, but it turned out that was a sideline with him. He was mainly president of Polaris Oil, which had started Husky 20-odd years before as a way of using up surplus gas. It also turned out how he and my mother had met. It was in Logan County, West Virginia, when she was a secretary for the Boone County Coal Corporation, at Clothier, and he was a young stockholder of Polaris, locating bus lines for them. He began taking charge of my life, how I should change my name to correspond, go to Cornell, to finish my college education, then move to Oklahoma to learn the ropes at Polaris, so I could succeed him as president when he felt he ought to retire. But I told him to back it up, that I'd decide those things, not he, and it made him laugh. But just to act friendly with him, I did agree to tape up all that happened, from the time Shaw came down until the inquest was over, so his secretary could type it up, and he would know everything. So I did, and this is it. Nothing's been settled yet, but I imagine I'll go to Cornell, and eventually head for Tulsa.

So that takes care of him, my mother, and me, but it doesn't take care of one other, and maybe a wedding we had, some weeks before my mother's. But to explain about her, and how one thing led to another, I'll have to backtrack a bit to that same afternoon after the officers left and we were all three sitting there—my mother, Jill, and me in the living room of my house—or at least my mother and I were, with Jill stretched out on the sofa. And my mother closed her eyes, saying: "How wonderful it would be if that phone were to ring right now, with the news I've been praying for. No, I don't pray for it, I wouldn't pray for somebody's death, but if it has to come, why couldn't it come now, so we could have it double, a real ceremony!"

"Double?" I asked her. "Double what?"

"Wedding, of course."

"Mother, if you're getting married, fine—I'll love it, and it'll be a wonderful day. But me, I'm not getting married, at all."

"You're damned right you're not—not to me anyway."

That was Jill, coming to life on the sofa. I said: "OK, Jill, that said it. Now how'd you like to get out?"

"I'll go when I get ready."

"You'll go now."

"*You'll* go and *kiss* her!" screamed my mother at me.

"Me and who else?"

Nobody moved, to go, kiss, or anything, but my mother let me have it. "You're just like your father!" she yelped, into my face. "Stubborn as a mule, one of those mules they have in Kentucky, that has to be hit with a chunk, a two-by-four scantling chunk, before you can get their attention and knock the stubbornness out! That stubbornness has kept me waiting for 20 years, because once he said we'd wait till that woman died out there, he was too bullheaded to switch! And fool that I am, I've waited and waited and waited, without finding myself any chunk. And she's still there and I'm still here and—you go over and kiss her, I say! You hear me?"

"I'm not deaf," I told her.

"*You!*" she bellowed at Jill. "Why aren't you finding a chunk? Why aren't you hitting him with it?"

"The chunks are all on the fire."

"You could bang him with that poke!"

But at that Jill jumped up. "I'm sick of the poke!" she screamed, bursting out crying again. "It's ruined them all—every last one that has touched it is dead, and it's not going to ruin me." She reached for the firescreen, pulled back when it burned her hands, then reached for the tongs, to topple it over with them. I suddenly realized she meant to heave that money right in the fire. That's when I grabbed it and flung her back on the sofa. "Oh no you don't!" I told her. "And there's not any jinx on it either—except for those who stole it, or tried to. For others it's perfectly good money, and that includes you. So take it and get out. It's yours, it's what you've been living for, praying for, and lying for—take it to bed at night, take its pants off and kiss it, and *once more, get the hell out!*"

I yanked her to her feet and gave her a boot in the tail. She whirled, perfectly furious, and let me have it in the head, with the bag, swinging it by the strap. I went out, seeing white lightning first. I was out a long time, and when I came to I was falling. I caught myself, staggered somehow to my feet, and started for her again. But her eyes opened wide, my lip suddenly tickled, and a blood spot showed on the floor. She hadn't hit me in the nose, but it was bleeding just the same. She came close, pushed me back on the sofa, and tilted my head back by raising my chin. My mother handed her a swatch of Kleenexes she got out of her handbag. Then she dived for the kitchen and came back with two clean dish towels, one wet. The wet one she put on my head, handing the other one to Jill. Jill jammed it under my nose and held it there, all the time sitting close, so I could feel how warm she was and how soft, especially her swellings in front. She kept whispering how sorry she was for those rotten things she had said: "But I wanted that money so—it was mine and I hated to lose it!" And then: "Bop me!"

"What?"

"I said, bop me."

She reached around behind, flipped her skirt up and slid down her panty hose, so her bottom was bare. "If you don't bop her," said my mother, "there's something wrong with you!"

I didn't bop her. I lay there with my eyes closed, wondering what her warmness, softness, and smell, which I could catch in her hair, had to do with what she had said, and how sore I was about it. I didn't have anything that I could see, and yet I didn't feel quite so sore any more. 'Stead of bopping, I patted her. Then my arm went around her. Then her mouth found mine. If you can't guess the rest. . . .